HELLFIRE

Book One of the Beyond Human Series

MICHELLE SCHAD

This book is a work of fiction. Names, characters, businesses, organizations, places, events and incidents either are the product of the author's imagination or are used fictitiously. Any resemblance to actual persons, living or dead, events, or locales is entirely coincidental.

For information contact :
http://www.tamingchaos.net

Book design by Michelle Schad
Cover Design by Black Bird Book Covers
ISBN: 9 7 8 0 9 9 8 2 6 0 5 3 2

1st Edition: April 2018 by Corrugated Sky Pub.
2nd Edition: December 2020

Chaos Publications

MORE FROM THE
BEYOND HUMAN SERIES

Hellfire
Evolved
Paradox
Transcendent

For all the heroes that don't wear capes.
Thank you.

For Mark, always.

For Matthew for all the reasons, all the wine, and all the unwavering support to soar.

To those that stand behind me, making my blanket cape flap in the imaginary wind, I cannot do any of this without you. You're amazing, you're appreciated, you are loved.

01

Hadi!

He coughed, choking on the rainwater that streamed down the sides of his broken nose. Each droplet dripped down the back of his throat along with the copper tang of his own blood.

Hadi!!

He took another gut punch to the stomach, curling in over the steel toe that delivered the painful blow. He wretched into the puddle beneath him, groaning pitifully after. The kicks continued, bruising his ribs, his sides and hips, his chest and back until he no longer had the strength to keep them away. Instead, he lay there, dead to the world around him, numb to the pain and hateful words spewed at him.

HADI!

The nightmare shattered like a broken window.

A violent hissing replaced the thunderous sound of falling rain. The taste and smell of copper evaporated into the odor of melting plastic.

"Get up!" someone barked in Arabic. The pain of the nightmare still lingered, but something about the barked order made Hadi Shahir's limbs move, made him sit up and force his eyes open. Half of his room was on fire.

"Shit," he cursed, immediately absorbing the flames into the palm of his hand. It burned the skin, reminding him of his curse. "Saleh, I'm sorry I-"

"You are late for work," his cousin, Saleh, said heavily. "Mary already called. She is waiting for you."

Hadi watched Saleh walk away with the fire extinguisher still in hand. The white foam was everywhere. There was absolutely nothing left of the television that once sat atop Hadi's dresser. He could hear Nima, Saleh's wife, asking if everything was all right as Saleh left the room and their baby girl crying from all the commotion Hadi caused.

The nightmare was the same every night.

Nothing he did made the memory of what was done to him go away. He tried alcohol and drugs, tried meditation or useless television, even bought himself a pet fish to see if it might offer some tranquility. The fish boiled the same week Hadi purchased it. The outcome of the nightmare was always the same, too: everything burned, including himself. Unfortunately, that meant everything in

[2]

the waking world burned too. His walls were a myriad of scorch marks and blackened outlines of furniture that no longer existed. Blessedly, the fires were always contained to his room, but it was only a matter of time before they tore free of the plywood door that separated Hadi from his cousin's family.

It took months for Hadi to recover from the physical trauma he endured. Mentally, however, he felt lost; adrift in a world that did not understand; did not *want* to understand. Saleh insisted he needed to find focus, put himself into his work, and push the nightmares away. The understanding and compassion Saleh had shown right after the incident slowly vanished to annoyance that Hadi simply could not just 'get over it'.

Hadi flinched when Saleh pounded on the bathroom door, demanding that he hurry up. The hot water felt good on Hadi's back, though; he did not want to leave. It cradled him in a much-needed embrace.

However, if he expected to get paid, he needed to walk the two blocks to the laundromat to watch over the empty washers and dryers while listening to late night television echo out into an empty establishment. No one came into the laundromat that Saleh owned after 10:00pm.

With a heavy heart and heavier feet, Hadi shrugged himself into his winter coat and shuffled out of the small apartment he shared with his cousin. It took a full five minutes to gain the courage to open the door to the building's foyer and set foot out onto the street. Two of the street lamps above flickered in a poor attempt to shed actual light onto the dirty sidewalk. He fought a wave of nausea and forced one foot in front of the other until he gained actual forward momentum. He hid inside his coat, stuffing hands deep into his pockets and scrunching down into the wool scarf around his face. His soft hair fell into his eyes or around his ears where it was not held back by a matching knit beanie. Winters in Chicago were brutal.

Hadi continued a little mantra while he walked the two-block distance from Saleh's apartment to the Wash n' Fluff laundromat that Saleh owned. His steps increased in speed as soon as he saw the sliding doors, all but running into the humid confines of the laundromat. Maria, the woman who worked the day shift, eyed him with annoyance and disapproval. She looked like everyone's grandmother but had the personality of a rusted spoon.

"*Lo siento*, Mary," Hadi intoned in horribly accented Spanish as the woman collected her things. She muttered something back, but he wasn't paying attention enough to hear it. He waited until she was gone to change the channel on the television and remove his coat, pulling a tiny baggie of white powder from the inside pocket. He took the baggie everywhere, catching a sniff any time he felt anxiety start to build up in his chest. It helped to relax his tense posture and racing mind, helped him to forget even if it was just for a few hours. The evening crawled along as most evenings did: in a blessed haze of psychedelic colors and nearly overwhelming heat. He dozed behind the cash counter where folks dropped off their bags of filthy clothes for the fluff and fold service the establishment offered.

He took quarters from the drawer to buy a soda

and chocolate bar from the vending machine, and 'skated' around the empty building inside one of the wheeled baskets that were kept in even rows just inside the front entrance. He read a book someone had left behind - *An Ember in the Ashes* by an author he had never head of - and then re-read the first chapter only two hours after finishing the book itself; he read fast. Eventually, boredom caught up to Hadi's over-active mind, the high wearing off too soon, and he fell asleep behind the cash counter.

"Hey," said a woman, rocking him off his chair and onto the floor. Something 'popped' behind him, smoldering briefly before he squashed the flame and scrambled to his feet. The woman - though she did not look much older than Hadi - grinned kindly. "Uhm, y'all are outta quarters."

Hadi blinked at the attractive young blond in tight leggings and chunky Ugg boots. She wore her hair in braids that fell over her shoulders with a slouchy knit beanie on her head and a sweater with too-long sleeves. 'Basic white girl' immediately jumped into his mind from something he had seen on social media. She fit the meme to a perfectly crossed T.

"Sorry - we don't leave the machine on after ten," Hadi explained finally in a barely audible croak before clearing his throat. "How much do you need?"

"Just five," she shrugged. "I don't got much to wash. You new 'round here?"

Hadi shook his head, unlocking the change drawer.

"No? You related to Sal? You kinda look like him," she continued, swaying a little as she spoke. Hadi glanced up at her, catching her very obvious flirtation and smirked.

"He's my cousin," Hadi grinned back, handing her the requested change. "You come in here a lot?"

She nodded. "I live just across the street so it's pretty easy. Normally I just drop off an' run but I didn't get to it today an' I'm outta underwear."

She bit her lower lip when she spoke, making Hadi's grin broaden. He gave her an appreciative glance, watching her walk back to her small basket of laundry. He practically died of a heart attack when his view was suddenly blocked by Saleh's imposing presence.

"Saleh," he breathed out. The girl at washer number four waved when Saleh looked at her but he did not wave back.

"You are lucky that I do not call the police," Saleh began. Hadi frowned in confusion but Saleh continued on. "I have protected you, hid your secrets from Nima and your father, and now you bring *this* into my home."

Saleh tossed a brown canvas sack onto the counter between them. Hadi's heart sunk, eyes closing as he exhaled slowly. He knew what was in the bag for it was the same type of contraband he had hidden in his coat pocket.

"You're fired," Saleh said. "Your things are outside."

"Saleh!" Hadi tried but the man would not hear it. His generosity only went so far and Hadi had finally set a fire he could not control.

~

[6]

Hadi sat around the corner of the Wash n'Fluff front entrance with a backpack on his shoulders and two garbage bags full of the few belongings he had not burned to a crisp. Saleh had been gracious enough to dole out his final paycheck in cash which meant Hadi had exactly three-hundred dollars to his name and whatever was in the bags at his feet. Anywhere decent would drain him of money and anywhere else set a twisted knot in the pit of his stomach to even think about. Cars rolled by, kicking up icy cold blasts of air and minuscule particles of dust. Some honked at each other, others blared loud music or ran from the sirens that chased them. Hadi, quite literally, had nowhere to go.

He called Chicago his home for a painfully short few months before the horrible incident that very nearly tore him apart occurred. He spent a great deal of time in the hospital and only knew mind-numbing 'work' since his recovery six months prior. His visa was under condition of study, yet he had no real interest in what the schools had to teach him. Much of what was taught was biased or so dull Hadi wanted to shoot himself in the foot just for some excitement. The *one* semester he managed to sit through was cut abruptly short when he argued with the professor regarding French history, something he was rather intimately familiar with.

France was his childhood home, where he grew up and learned the most but the professor in question only saw him as an obstruction and kicked him out the very same night of the argument. Saleh put him to work shortly thereafter, and then terror in a dark alley robbed Hadi of everything else. Now he didn't even have mind- numbing work and no way to get back home either.

"Didn't sound like things went too well when Sal came in," the girl from washer four said. Hadi looked up at her. She held her laundry basket in her arms, a big puffy coat protecting her from the elements. He didn't know what to say so remained silent, looking back down at his booted feet instead. "What's your name, handsome?"

Hadi looked up at her again and blinked curiously. "Hadi. Shahir."

"Lindsay-Rae," she replied with a smile and gentle sway. "Everyone just calls me Lindy, though. Let's go, Hadi Shahir."

He frowned at her, standing uncertainly so that he practically towered over her. "Go?"

"You're just like a lost little puppy and I'm not one what lets strays sit out in the cold. Folks don't sit out on street corners with trash bags o' junk if they've got some place to stay. C'mon."

Hadi opened his mouth to say something but nothing emerged save a pathetic croak. He glanced at the glowing light coming from the Wash n'Fluff, then back at Lindy. It took less than half a second for him to heft the two trash bags up and trot across the street after the 'basic white girl' with the unwashed under garments.

"Why?" Hadi asked as he finally caught her up.

"Why what?" Lindy asked, unlocking the front door to her apartment on the second floor.

"Why help me? You don't even know me."

Lindy shrugged. "You're cute. And I'm kinda hopin' you can cook better than I can. I could use food that don't come from a bar."

The smile she gave him lightened the weight that pressed down upon him considerably. He grinned back, snorting a little with the loosening he felt in his chest and shoulders.

"I hope that you like macaroni and cheese," Hadi teased. To Hadi's credit, he knew how to cook a rather large array of things. It was something his mother taught him despite his father's disapproval at such things. Cooking, he would say, was women's work. All the same, both Hadi and his younger brother learned to cook by sheer observation and some devious test runs when no one else was in the house. And, despite an egregious amount of laziness, Hadi also knew how to keep a house clean - something Lindy seemed to be lacking entirely.

So, for the first week, Hadi played home maker to his new friend. The extra perks were nice as well. She never judged him for his habits and, more often than not, joined him in a sniff or two or shared a joint on the fire escape stairs. She also had a blessedly insatiable appetite for the flesh that Hadi was more than willing to tackle. It kept his mind off the dire straights he was in or the nightmares that crept into his mind when no one was around. While he was eternally grateful to Lindy for her caring heart, he knew he could not stay with her forever.

It was a conundrum he pondered while lying on the sofa. The TV to his right ran through reruns of *The X-Files,* making the darkness in the room almost eerie with the awkward shadows and creepy sounds. Hadi did his best to ignore it, blowing out a stream of pungent smoke into the air above him. His muscles relaxed, arm dropping lazily to the carpeted floor. The joint rolled into the palm of his hand as he drifted off to fitful sleep.

Hadi!

He coughed, choking on rainwater. There was a pain in the palm of his hand that seemed out of place, dull and throbbing but agonizing at the same time.

Hadi!!

This time, Hadi's eyes snapped open with a sharp intake of breath. There was no rain, no dark alley, or mocking voices. There was only the dark living room of Lindy's apartment and the drifting noise from the TV. It was then, he realized, that Lindy sat on the floor beside him, massaging his right hand. His whole palm felt raw, making him hiss and pull away.

"You ok?" she asked when he pulled his hand away. The center of his palm was scorched, marred in black and red with tiny ashes practically welded to his skin.

"Yeah…" he breathed out, sitting up. He ran his good hand through his hair, pulling the other close to his chest. "Yeah, sorry."

Lindy stared at him, big eyes full of concern and a touch of fear. He'd done something; he could tell by the way she stared, the way she stayed rooted to the spot on the floor. He could not smell anything, and nothing looked damaged even in the dark. He'd not been asleep for very long.

"Bad dream?" Lindy asked gently, cautiously. He glanced at her and nodded. "You're one of 'em, aren't you?"

Again, Hadi glanced at her, feeling a knot form in his stomach and his throat clench. Lindy looked down at her lap, and then pulled his right hand towards her so that they could both see the blackened mark on his palm.

"It was on fire," she explained. "Your hand. It was on fire. I read about folks like you. They talk about 'em on TV sometimes."

Hadi felt his mouth drop open as if to explain or deny her accusation. Instead, it just hung open until he sighed and turned away, pulling his hand back away from her.

"What happened?" she persisted, daring to scoot a little closer. "You twitch sometimes when we're in bed; and you're a great cook but you're always high, Hadi. What're you hidin' from?"

It was not something Hadi wanted to recount because it meant he had to relive it. And yet, he could not stop the words from falling off his tongue. He told her. He told her about the young man he met at a club not long after arriving in the states, how beautiful his smile was and how much he liked to dance; Emmet was his name. He told her how angry Saleh had been when he learned where Hadi was going at night. He told her about the men that dragged him and Emmet into an alley, how they had both screamed for help but no one heard over the roar of the storm. He told her how they beat Emmet to death and nearly done the same to him. He told her how the police looked for clues, asked some questions, but, ultimately, let the case go unsolved. He told her how he had not been able to sleep since then, or walk the streets at night without wanting to vomit. He told her how every time he felt afraid, something always caught fire and how, sometimes - most times - he wished the flames would just eat him alive.

02

Sunlight directly to the face woke Hadi the following morning. His head felt fogged over and the palm of his hand throbbed something fierce. Not much else would surface to memory, however, so he simply groaned and let his head fall back to the pillows. The vibrating buzz of a phone pulled him further from cotton-headed sleep until he slapped the small little rectangle to his left. Left?

Hadi lifted his head up enough to peer at his surroundings. It was not the sofa on which he slept, nor was it the living room. He frowned at that, at the tiny little pink rosebuds on the sheets that covered his naked body while still holding on to the vibrating phone. His right hand was wrapped in soft white gauze that was slowly staining itself pink. There were kitten posters on the walls or full-length images of bands Hadi was not familiar with. Lindy's room.

"Yeah?" he croaked into the phone while staring

at the side table where the phone had been. A tiny plastic baggie of white powder stared back, its mouth wide open and spilling snow-white dust all over the table's surface. Well, that explained things. "Lindy?"

He could hear the excitement in his roommate's voice. She spoke faster than his addled mind could process, however, making him roll to a seated position on her bed and scratch at his head. "Wait, wait… say that again. - - I just woke up. - - Shut up. - - No, no bad dreams last night. Thanks."

Lindy continued on, repeating her exuberant words into his ear. She wanted to meet him for lunch at a bar called the 13th Hour; the same bar she worked at, if he recalled correctly. All things considered, despite living with the woman, he still knew very little about her. All the same, he promised to shower and meet her within the hour. So, true to his word, Hadi forced compliance from his limbs, washed up, re-wrapped his burned hand, and caught a cab to the bar in question.

It was not terribly far from where Lindy lived as cabs went. The inside of the bar was dimly lit with industrial-looking lamps hanging from the ceiling. Booths and high tables filled the open space with a juke box against one wall, and darts on the other. There was a large, flat screen TV above the juke box running day time television as he walked in, the tiny bell above the door jingling loudly in his ears.

"Hey!" Lindy said as Hadi walked in. She bounced to him, hugging him tightly as if all the depressing talk the night before had never occurred. "Tam, this is Hadi, the guy I was just tellin' you about."

Hadi arched a questioning brow as Lindy dragged him over to the bar. She introduced him to Tamara Marshall, owner and proprietor of the 13th Hour as well as the building manager. The woman was easily in her forties, handsome, with chocolate skin and bleached braids tied up in a loose bun at the nape of her neck. She nodded at him while cleaning the bar down with a wet rag that smelled of bleach and peanuts.

"Lindy says you're looking for a job," Tam said to him. No-nonsense, to the point. Hadi glanced at Lindy but nodded in the affirmative. "Ever wait tables?"

"No," he answered honestly. "I learn quick though."

"Can you mix a drink?" the owner continued, eying him up and down as if he were about to be sold to the highest bidder. Hadi swallowed the sudden rise in nerves, clenched his hurt hand shut so tight he was sure he made it bleed and nodded. "Show me. Make me a tequila sunrise."

Hadi blinked. Again, he looked at Lindy who gave him the most blessedly reassuring smile anyone ever shot his way. He cleared his throat, removing his coat as he squeezed in behind the bar and took a quick look at the impressive stock of liquor on the shelves. They had almost every hard liquor known to man and seven beers on tap. He didn't bother looking inside the beer fridge, already imagining how full that would be. Instead, he bit down on his lower lip and collected the bottles needed for a tequila sunrise. When he was finished, he hesitated, wiping his hands on his pants and then slid the drink across the bar to

Tamara.

"I don't see any cherries or orange slices out," he explained softly. Tamara arched a brow, smirking as she sniffed at the drink and took a sip. Hadi watched her savor the drink, then slide it across to Lindy.

"Dirty martini."

Hadi opened his mouth to question but thought better of it. Just like with the tequila sunrise, he gathered what he could easily find, including the olives this time though he had to ask for those, and mixed the drink, pouring it into a chilled martini glass. Tamara savored the drink in the same way she did the first, conferring silently across the bar with Lindy.

"You're hired," Tamara said after a very long stint of contemplative silence. "You can start tomorrow. Lindy will train you. I got two rules: don't come to my work high and don't steal from me. If you can follow those rules, we'll be cool. You break those rules, and I'll turn your ass out faster than you can blink. Are we clear?"

"Yes," Hadi said, mouth hanging slightly open. Tamara merely nodded and finished off the martini with one long gulp giving a satisfied sigh after. She winked at Lindy and left the pair alone, sliding back into the kitchens. Lindy practically bounced out of her seat with excitement.

"She rents the apartments upstairs too. There ain't none open now but when there is one, I don't doubt she'll let you have one. Not that I'm kickin' you out or nothin' but, I wager you're gonna want your own place eventually."

Hadi smiled and kissed her cheek by way of

thanks. It wasn't much, but it was a start.

~

Hadi smiled, raising his hand to the poor old drunk that stumbled out the door between uniformed police officers. It was the same every night for Greg since Hadi began working; since the bar had opened according to everyone else. The man drank too much whiskey, ate too little food, and proceeded to fall over. Twice Hadi called the ambulance to take him to a hospital; most times, the local patrol that passed through for dinner would take him to a halfway house or a holding cell at the station until Greg sobered up.

The officers waved as well, as familiar now with Hadi as they were with Greg. He wiped the bar down with a fresh rag and restocked glasses, noting the time on the clock behind the bar.

"Hey, Moose," Hadi called into the kitchen as he returned the empty glass crates to the stack beside the washer. "Throw the onion brick on, yeah? V should be in soon."

"Sure thing, Haze," the giant cook said. He was easily two of Hadi, tall and broad with skin as dark as coal and eyes that saw everything. He was no good with names at all, giving everyone he met a nickname that was easier for him to recall. Hadi was dubbed 'Hazel' thanks to the color of his eyes the very first night he worked. Eventually, the name evolved into 'Haze', which was equally fitting. He kept his promise to Tamara and never set foot into the bar when it was his shift while high. Off-shift, well, he had come in on cloud nine a few times to pick up Lindy. The day he moved into his own apartment required a hefty dosing of hallucinogenics too that Lindy shared with him before dragging him down for dinner at the bar. The nightmares lingered, though they were more manageable than before. He called Lindy any time he had one, listening to her voice until he stopped trembling. So far, nothing had burned; nothing important anyway. Books, or pieces of paper went up into a pile of blackened ashes, but that was as far as the fires got. Lindy kept his secret, kept their relationship casual with benefits, and kept him sane.

"HAZE!!" Hadi heard from the kitchen and smiled. Moose shook his head, marveling at the timing Hadi had. He walked back out to the dining area, arms raised in a 'V' for the man that now sat at the bar. If Moose was big, Virgil Kriskin was enormous. The man was an ex-con. Hadi didn't know where he worked or what he did when he was not in the bar, but he was good people. He had a quirky sense of humor, and loved wrestling like men loved women. "Ha, my man!"

"Hey, V," Hadi replied, pouring a stout from draft. "Ring brick's in the fryer."

"Love it, love it," Virgil nodded, reaching for the remote so he could change the channel. The other two people in the bar hardly cared. "How you settling in the new digs?"

"Ok," Hadi shrugged. "Still got too many boxes. I started with two bags of stuff, you know? Dunno how I ended up with a whole place of cardboard."

Virgil laughed, a throaty sound that was infectious. "Cuz you let a woman help you buy shit you don't need!"

Hadi only rolled his eyes and smiled, heading back to the kitchen to retrieve Virgil's log of onion crisps. They weren't really rings and if there were actually onions in the log, Hadi would forsake pot for a month, but they tasted like onion rings which is what mattered to Virgil.

"Hey, Haze, think you can relight the pilot under the stove when you're done droppin' that brick off? I ain't got skinny arms like you; can't reach it," Moose asked.

"Sure, gimme a sec ok?" Hadi replied, taking the grease-filled brick of onion curls out to Virgil. "Onion brick."

"You are a saint, Haze. For real. Got the-"

Virgil cut off as Hadi set down a bottle of ketchup, a bottle of A-1 Steak sauce, and a bottle of Tabasco. All three condiments found their way onto the brick every time Virgil came in.

"You're a gem," Virgil said with a bright smile. "Thanks, my man."

Hadi laughed, heading back into the kitchen. The stove's pilot was all the way at the back of the oven - well, *under* the back of the oven. The giant beast of a machine was old as dirt. He'd seen Tam and Lindy both crawling underneath it's greasy under belly to relight the pilot on many occasions. Moose handed him a pack of matches, moving stuff aside so Hadi could wrench himself beneath the stove unobstructed.

"This thing gonna blow up on me?" Hadi teased as he squeezed and stretched.

"God, I hope not. I keep tellin' Tam we need a new one but she's gonna keep squeezin' all she can out of it."

That did not make Hadi feel much better. He lit the match with a flick of his thumb once his arm was out of sight of Moose's gaze. It went out twice with no contact to the pilot. Hadi cursed under his breath, rolling onto his belly instead with a new match. Again, he flicked his thumb over the match head, watching it light up in bright orange. This time, it caught - and kept going.

"Shit," Hadi spat, trying to contain the flame. It only spread further, snaking up the gas line and across the grease stuck to the underside of the oven. "Moose! Moose!"

The giant cook yanked on Hadi's ankles, tugging him out from beneath the stove as the entire thing went up in a burst of flame that shook the pans right off their hooks.

"Holy shit, Haze - you ok?" Moose asked, though the flame was not contained, not in the least.

"Out, out!" Hadi ordered, shoving the larger man out into the dining area as the stove hissed. Three seconds later, it burst like an over taxed tea-kettle, sending flames roaring up to the ceiling or across the floor towards Hadi's feet. Instinct kicked in. He opened up to the flames that reached for him and sucked them into his palms, rolling the fire into a ball that was easier to contain. He fell backwards when Moose ran back into the kitchen with a fire extinguisher, his concentration lost. It was enough though. The fire extinguisher did the trick. Hadi heard one of the bar patrons talking to the fire department, giving them the address of the bar.

"You ok, kiddo?" Virgil said, hefting Hadi to his feet. Hadi winced, hissing in pain. His elbow was red and his right palm was a scorched mess; again. "That don't look good. Put some vanilla on it."

"What?" Hadi said, looking at the much larger man curiously. Moose continued to spray the stove with the fire extinguisher, some of the grease still trying to hold on to a weak flame. The fire alarms were blaring all over the bar and the dinning room sprinklers spit out a pathetic spray of water over the tables and booths.

"Yeah," Virgil nodded. "Works better than aloe. You're gonna need to get that looked at though. You're lucky that stove didn't fry you to a crisp like my onion brick."

"Yeah, no shit," Hadi sighed.

"You're good people, Haze," Virgil said, rubbing his shoulders rather roughly. "That was brave what you did. Dumb as shit, but brave."

"I didn't do anything," Hadi breathed out. Virgil only snorted, slapping him on the back with enough force to hurt. Tam was going to get her new stove now whether she wanted it or not.

"Right, and I'm just big and tall," Virgil grinned. "People like us, we're some kind of special. Ask my parole officer."

Hadi merely groaned.

03

Agent Valerie Banrae of the Agency for Evolved Control, also known simply as Sparrow, squatted with the grace of a hunting lion amongst the char and violence laid out before her.

Twelve people all turned into corpse-shaped pieces of charcoal. Several other people moved about the crime scene, with a ring of A.E.C. agents keeping back curious onlookers or media personnel. The Agency for Evolved Control was in place to prevent things like this senseless massacre from happening. For the most part, they kept things in check, helping the Evolved that needed it and incarcerating those that used their natural born gifts against mankind and, most importantly, keeping it all silent. But, sometimes, the level of sadistic fuck-face was just too high. This was one of those times.

"Sparrow."

Valerie stood up, her honey blond hair whipping back into her face as she turned to face the woman that spoke to her. Zephyr, a highly trained Agent of the A.E.C.'s most elite, outranked her despite being several decades younger. She was a member of the PeaceKeepers, an Evolved herself, and highly respected both in the states and abroad. Valerie walked up to the petite woman in a tailored suit and harlequin mask, eying the other woman that stood beside her in full blacks with a mask to cover her face as well; secrets.

"We just got word that there was another fire within city limits," Zephyr nearly growled, her accented English clipping with propriety and annoyance. "A bar. But we're not there to investigate. Why?"

"I hadn't heard. It might not be related," Sparrow said, peering at the younger woman and her companion.

"If and when I decide something is not related to this horseshit, it will mean I have a tag on my pinky toe and failed to resurrect! Until further notice, *all* fires within the greater Chicago metropolitan area are related, is that understood?"

"Yes, ma'am," Sparrow nodded.

"Get someone down there and find out what happened."

"Yes, ma'am," Sparrow repeated, sneering as she turned away from the younger woman. Tart.

She understood the frustration, but the attitude was unnecessary. There was nothing left of the duplex that housed four families. Every single one perished. There were no signs of an accelerant, yet the fire obviously spread quickly and at high temperatures. Things were melted together, the bodies fallen from beds or chairs where they had been prior to the fire. There had been no time for escape. Whoever did this, was an Evolved with immense power. Moreover, whoever they were, they'd been setting fires across the whole of the Chicago metropolitan area for over four years now. It was starting to get frustrating.

"Duck!" Sparrow barked. A man with black hair and Ray-Ban sunglasses trotted over to her along with three other black-suited agents. They were absurd, always flocking in small packs, but they knew how to do their job. "Bar fire couple nights ago - go figure it out. I want names. I want incident reports from the police. I want suspects, gentlemen. We're looking for an Evolved. Get on it."

"Sure thing," Duck replied. He jerked his head towards the others who peeled away while she watched. Their entire agency worked off of secrecy and code names. Duck seemed like such an absurd name until she observed how he interacted with the other goons that followed - all like a flock of ducks traveling for the season. Sparrow shook her head and checked her phone. Two messages from her mother and the expected check- in from her parolee. "Good job, Virgil. Keep up the good work…"

~

Hadi glanced up at Lindy and Tamara, both enamored with the young man that sat between them. Amir, his younger brother, arrived earlier that morning. His energy and enthusiasm for the States spread like a plague, making the women swoon or giggle while Hadi mixed early afternoon drinks for the lot of them before the bar opened for the dinner rush.

"I had never been on a plane. I thought that I was going to die!" Amir laughed, gripping his heart in dramatic fashion. The two women laughed; Hadi shook his head. He was glad to have Amir around. The two were so close, that not having him around for the past year made life seem surreal. Much like Hadi when he first arrived, Amir was now in the States on a student visa to finish his master's degree at the University of Chicago.

The 13th Hour was a little darker than normal despite the light fixtures hanging from the ceiling. Several had popped during the stove incident, a backlash of Hadi's power that he had not accounted for until none of the stupid things would turn on. The insurance company still fought Tamara on replacing the stove, claiming user error rather than faulty equipment. Every time Hadi walked back into the kitchen, he felt guilty for the trouble he had caused her but he tried to shove that aside in favor of enjoying his brother's arrival.

"... would. Not. Stop. Screaming. It was, like, someone turned the volume up on that dammed kid. *Like, Mara, yeah?*"

"What'd he say?" Tam asked with a smirk on her full lips unable to understand the last part of Amir's statement.

"Like Mara," Hadi translated. "Our sister. She's sixteen. She used to scream a lot."

"Still does," Amir groaned. They all laughed.

The door opened at that point, the tiny bell jingling wildly as three men in sharp suits entered the bar. They looked like they belonged at a fancy bar as bouncers or, perhaps, following the president on her daily jogs through wherever the news reported that she jogged through. Or maybe the Men in Black. Either way, they did not belong inside the 13th Hour.

"Sorry, fellas, we're closed until 4:00p," Tamara said. The men did not move, the one in front with rich black hair pulling out a badge that only gave a few seconds of flashing brass for them to look at and nothing more.

"We're here to ask a few questions ma'am," he said brusquely. "There was a fire here a few days ago, yes?"

Tamara frowned and crossed her arms beneath her breasts. "My stove blew up. Thing was old as dirt, we're lucky the whole building didn't go up."

"Hadi Shahir?" Black Hair said, ignoring Tamara completely. "My report says you were here the night of the fire - is that correct?"

"Yes," Hadi said calmly. Tamara's nostrils flared in fury. She did not like being ignored.

"Mind if we talk, Hadi?" the suit with black hair suggested. Hadi folded his arms across his chest and smirked.

"We are talking."

They did not like that answer, two of the three arching brows while Lindy and Amir bit back grins of mirth. Hadi did not move from his spot, however. The badges that the men flashed were not police or FBI; Hadi watched enough television or read plenty to know what those looked like. Whoever they were, they were not actually there for the stove.

"Hadi, how long have you lived here, in the States?" Black Hair asked. He stepped further into the bar, removing his Ray-Ban sunglasses. He had dark, piercing eyes and eyebrows in desperate need of a good weed whacker. The other two stood their ground, present for effect rather than necessity.

"Almost two years, I guess," Hadi shrugged.

"You have proper documentation, I assume."

"I sponsor his work visa," Tamara interrupted. "What is this about, gentlemen?"

"This says you have dual citizenship in France and … Iran," Black Hair continued, still ignoring Tamara. Even Lindy and Amir noticed, both of them losing their mirth in favor of annoyed, defensive frowns.

"I do. I was born in Iran. We moved to France right after my brother turned one so I know France more than Iran. My parents and sister are still there."

"Is that your brother?"

Hadi glanced at Amir but refused to offer an answer, narrowing his eyes at the idiot with Burt Brows.

"Gentlemen," Tamara interjected, rising to her feet. She effectively blocked the path between Black Hair and Hadi. "Unless you're here to take pictures of my busted up stove - which is sittin' out back, mind - or to ask about the actual *fire* that nearly blew my staff up, I suggest you take your leave. I won't have no one harassing my employees just cuz they wearing fancy suits and ties with your knock-off Ray-Bans."

"Ma'am this is part of an ongoing investigation,"

Black Hair tried.

"My big tits it is," Tamara cut in. "I am a very strong and confident black woman, Mr. Ray-Bans but I know racial profiling when I see it. You're not here for my stove. Now I don't care what you think you came in here for, I'm done entertaining your stupidity. Please leave before I call the cops."

"Ma'am, our jurisdiction supersedes the local police." Black Hair sighed. Hadi remained placid. Tamara was a nettle of thorns. Poor Lindy only looked concerned as did Amir; he'd only just arrived.

"Tam," Hadi said easily. "It's ok. Guys, have I done something wrong?"

"That's what we're here to determine, Mr. Shahir," Black Hair replied. "Where were you last night?"

"Working," Hadi said calmly though he felt his stomach twist in knots all the same.

"Can anyone corroborate that?" Black Hair asked. Hadi arched a brow.

"I can," Lindy replied. "We was both here 'til 'bout 4am."

"And after?" Black Hair pressed. "Can anyone account for your whereabouts after 4am, Mr. Shahir?"

"What is this about?" Hadi asked.

"Just answer the question, sir," Black Hair insisted. Now, Hadi was angry. He could feel the burn at the pit of his stomach and swallowed hard against the desire to light the asshole's pants on fire.

"We was upstairs, ya manner-less asshole," Lindy continued. She stood as well, planting hands on hips.

"Your momma must've had a field day with you. Shoulda taught you better manners - and how to manscape. You got somethin' wild goin' on in your brow area there; hope it's not the same in your pants. *But* for your insistent information, I helped Hadi get his brother's room ready after work, we fucked - since you seem to want juicy detail - went to get pancakes at Maddison's - go 'head an' ask her, cuz she waited on us personal - then went to the airport to pick up his brother; in *my* car 'fore you ask. We brought Amir back home, took a nap, fucked *again,* and then came here for lunch. Do you need more detail than that for your recordin' device you got in your pocket or are ya good?"

Black Hair had nothing to say. Hadi palmed his face, feeling his face go so red he very nearly burst into flames on the spot. The other two standing with Black Hair cleared their throats nervously and stared at the floor.

"No," Black Hair finally conceded. "No, that'll do. If we have more questions, we'll call on you."

"Doubt it," Lindy intoned with full Texas sass behind her words.

The three men turned and left, practically stepping over themselves to get away. Once the bell had stopped jingling, Tamara turned to face Lindy, hands on hips as well and smirked.

"Lindsay-Rae Michaels," she scolded gently. "You kiss your momma with that tongue, missy?"

"Momma's dead - Jesus rest her lovin' soul," Lindy threw back. "Kiss my daddy though. The hell they think they are?"

"A.E.C.," Tamara sighed. "S'all I need. Boy, I love

you like you was my own. You're good people, but if you got a secret I need to know about, spill it now 'fore I got more of them assholes rolling up into my place of business."

"A.E.C.?" Amir asked.

"Agency for Evolved Control," Tamara said while looking directly at Hadi. How or why she knew the acronym was not something Hadi was willing to ask. She fixed him with a look that made the temperature drop at least five degrees. He swallowed hard, glanced over at the door, then at Amir, and finally snapped his fingers. A small flame burst to life in the palm of his scarred hand, dancing in blue and orange hues. He did not let it linger long, extinguishing the flame almost as soon as it rippled to life. Tamara only stared for a moment, releasing a long sigh as she hung her head between her shoulders.

"Ok," she said. "Ok…"

"Tam…" Hadi began. His stomach was in so many knots he felt nauseated. He wanted to apologize or explain but Tamara held up her hand and forestalled him.

"I don't wanna know, Hadi," she said, using his actual name rather than the nickname that had become so normal for him to hear. "Lord Jesus, I do not want to know. Now, you're gonna pour me a glass of bourbon and we're gonna forget this ever happened. You've been good to us so I will return the favor, but boy, you bring trouble to my door…"

"I won't, Tam, I'm-"

Tamara held her hand up again, cutting Hadi off. She only shook her head and gestured for the drink she requested. He gave it to her just how she liked it: two ice cubes, tumbler half full. She drank it all in one gulp, the ice cubes clattering in the glass as she set it back down on the bar.

"Your shift starts at six tonight," Tamara said. "Joey's got a part in the school play. Don't blow up any more of my stoves. Welcome to America, Amir."

Tamara said nothing else, shaking her head as she left the bar. Hadi wanted to hide under a rock. Both Lindy and Amir stared at him with mixed concern and sympathy on their faces but the damage was already done.

They knew his secret.

They knew what he was.

~

Sparrow pillowed her head against her folded arms while Duck delivered his report. Angelo Gustavo, also known as Duck, was a decent enough agent, but not the best at interrogation. He was too gruff, lacked a certain finesse required when dealing with Evolved. Most were secretive about their abilities, fearing retaliation from loved ones or neighbors if their secret was known. Yes, there were a few public figures like Zephyr or Ronin - both of whom stood in the crisp white room while Duck delivered his report - but, for the most part, Evolved were just normal folks with a terrible curse on their heads.

The antiseptic brightness of the room made Sparrow's head throb. Duck's droning voice made it worse. He was over-zealous and quick to jump to conclusions. No finesse at all.

"...rather protective of him," Duck concluded. "I

think they're hiding something. He's definitely-"

"Some poor kid you probably just scared the piss out of, Duck," Sparrow groaned.

"Are you suggesting the girl's story checks out?"

"Duck," Sparrow said, sitting up with her hair falling in her face. "A woman will not expressly admit to *fucking* unless she's angry with you, in which case, she's not going to lie about the act and wouldn't use that vernacular unless you've really pissed her off."

"She's got a point," Zephyr said. Her British accent still grated on Sparrow's nerves but, oddly enough, it was fitting for the woman in Valkyrie armor as opposed to the woman in the tailored suit. "He may be Evolved - and will need to be watched - but he didn't set the fire last night. That doesn't mean he's off the hook."

"Agent Falcon is on his way in from Arizona," Sparrow explained. She worked with James Kendall before; they were close. Many teased them for having a relationship, something expressly *not* allowed amongst fellow agents, but it was only a tease. It was because of James that Valerie met her late husband. Patrick insisted that James stand in as Valerie's 'man of honor' during their wedding. It was James who talked to her every night and virtually tucked in her children now that their father was finally at rest. Yes, they were close. Valerie needed him nearby now when things were so chaotic in Chicago.

"James Kendall," Zephyr read off a dossier in her hand that Duck provided. Overly thorough prick. "Former military. No family? You're listed as his next of kin, Agent Sparrow."

"James and I are close," Valerie explained, daring to use his actual name in front of others in the agency; it was not normally done. "He's like my brother. He's an only child, both parents deceased. We were recruited together."

"There's a red flag on his medical record," Zephyr pointed out, looking to Valerie for an explanation. Sparrow glared at the brown-haired Brit. "Is he fit for duty?"

"He's fit," Sparrow said. "He was diagnosed with MS five years ago. It hasn't impeded his work, and he is regularly checked out by A.E.C. physicians. I don't even know why that's in there."

"Because it needs to be," Zephyr snipped back, snapping the dossier closed. "I want to speak with him when he arrives. Duck, set him up in the building across from this bar you went to - almost all of them in this gods awful city have tenement housing above the shops."

The woman in all black, known as Ronin, said something in Japanese. Sparrow couldn't understand her but she very obviously understood English. Now she *really* wished James were there with her. He spoke almost everything.

"Because the young man Duck failed to interrogate is still an Evolved, and most likely a fire manipulator. Until we have proof otherwise, he sits on the top of the suspect list. I want Agent Falcon on him like white on rice. The rest of you, find me that bloody fire manipulator. There's got to be more than one in this city. Flush them out."

04

"**J**ust be careful how you handle it, Val," James said as he stood on the sidewalk in front of his new apartment building. He held a pack of Camels in his hand, pounding them as any good nicotine addict would, his cell phone tucked into his back pocket and Bluetooth ear piece blinking steadily in the waning light. "Yeah, I know his history, that's why I'm telling you to be careful. Duck's screwed things up more than he's made them better and he doesn't really take kindly to women giving him orders unless it's the ho from San Diego. For Christ's sake his call sign is *Duck*. - - I didn't pick it. - - Fuck that, I wanted your name. - - Berase Falcon is copywritten, and not a Pirate. - - Uh, since forever. Who wouldn't want to be a pirate? - - No, I got my truck unloaded this afternoon. It's box city up there right now. The rest of it doesn't come in until Wednesday. - - Yeah, that's next on my list. I don't even have ketchup. - - Heh,

nah, I'll be good. The bar across the street looks promis-
ing. - - Well that's where this guy works, right? Might as
well get a jump on things. Don't got nothing better to do.
Can't believe we're dealing with two of these bastards. - -
What? No, I'm not smoking. - - No.- - I'm not smoking!
Shit, woman... - - Never. Seriously, though, I'm glad to be
here. I've missed you. - - Love you too; kiss those kids for
me. - - Later."

James Kendall finished pounding out the new pack
of Camels before popping one of the cancerous sticks out
of the fresh packaging. He hadn't lied to Valerie; mostly.
He lit up as he jaywalked across the street to the bar with
the rustic-looking sign that read "13th Hour" in neon blue
with the curve of the lower case 'h' burned out. He could
smell the food from across the street, delicious scents of
deep-fried onions and greasy burgers. He wanted it all
after the work he'd put in that day. Everything he brought
with him was on the third floor of a brick building in the
East Side district of Chicago. It was probably more than he
should have done, all things considered. He could feel the
twitch in his right arm, forcing his hand to flex a few times
as he smoked his beloved cigarette. There were too many
differences from Arizona. The weather, for one, was a bit
too cold for James's liking and the wind was killer. 'Windy
City' was an understatement in his opinion.

Still, it was now 'home' so he would endure as he
did when he'd been moved to the sweltering Hell hole of
no-man's-land Arizona.

He finished off his cigarette, giving his cell phone
one last check to make sure things had not changed as he

crushed the smoldering butt into the pavement before en-
tering the 13th Hour. A tiny bell above the door jingled as
he entered the bar. It was dimly lit with booths and a few
high tables. The bar itself was long, wrapping around the
back end of the establishment with an impressive collection of liquor bottles on wood shelves. There were a few
patrons, each of them too entrenched in their own conversations or lives to bother with James. He didn't mind at
all, swinging himself over one of the barstools a few seats
down from an elderly gentleman with a tumbler full of
bourbon.

"Shut up!" a young man said as he came from the
double doors to the kitchen carrying a plate laden with a
heaping pile of French fries and two onion rings. He set
them down in front of the elderly gentleman and smiled.
"Fries and onion rings, as requested."

"Thanks, Haze," the man slurred. The bartender nodded then looked towards James. He had the most
stunning hazel colored eyes and dark olive skin. It was an
enticing contrast that made James flush in spite of himself.
He was here for dinner, not a date.

"A new face to my bar," the bartender said. "Curious. What'll it be, new face?"

"James," he offered. "Guiness. On draft, if you've
got it."

"If I've got it," the bartender said in mock offense.
He pulled a chilled glass from a freezer and poured out the
requested drink like a pro, setting it down in front of James
with a smile. "From where do you come, James?"

"Arizona," James answered, enjoying the conversation with another human being. It had been a very long and boring drive.

"Ugh, too hot," the bartender groaned, waving it all off as if doing so would banish the state back into the pits of Hell where it belonged. "Work move?"

James grinned and nodded, taking a blessedly long drink from his glass. It was the best beer he'd had in a long time. Logically, he knew that was a lie but in that moment it was exactly what he needed.

"HAZE!"

The booming voice made James look over his shoulder. A beast of a man walked in, arms raised in a 'V' that was mimicked by the bartender.

"My man!" the newcomer bellowed.

"I'll get your brick into the fryer right now, V," the bartender said.

"No, no - think I'm gonna change it up a bit. Parole officer says I need to change my diet."

"Wait, wait, wait - MOOSE!" the bartender hollered as he pulled his phone out of his pocket and aimed it at the newcomer. All the other patrons stopped to watch the debacle as well, some smiling or whispering as they waited. Another very large man, this one dark of skin and much older, came out of the kitchens with a greasy towel in hand and an apron wrapped around his girth. "Ok, V, go 'head."

"Serious?" the man named V said. He looked at James who only offered a shrug, smirking at the antics around him. The bartender was his target, he knew that much, but, so far, the kid was just that - a kid, probably no older than twenty-four with a lot of regulars he seemed to genuinely care about. "*Any*way, so Banrae said I'll die of a coronary before my parole's up if I keep eating them bricks. So... I'm switchin' to fries. Potatoes are a vegetable, right?"

The entire bar burst out laughing. Even James had to chuckle despite hearing Valerie's name. The beast of a man was one of Valerie's parolees. Good grief! He hoped she never had to deal with *that* during a tirade.

The cook went back into the kitchen to get the fries while jokingly commenting that he would add some parsley to the plate so there was something green on it. The bartender punched the order in, still chuckling and smiling, when he turned back to check on James.

"Hungry? Or you good making love to your beer?" the bartender asked. James laughed. He liked the guy. His words had a slight accent to them that was hard to place: not quite French but enough of it to make James think that at least part of him was French or else he'd spent a great deal of time there. He hadn't read the full dossier yet.

"God, I'd kill for a burger and fries," James admitted. He knew that he probably would too, if it really came down to it. His stomach agreed, rumbling loudly right at that moment. "See?"

The bartender laughed as he turned to punch in the order on the touch-screen register behind him. "Everything on it?"

"Yes, please," James said, taking another long drink of his beer. He let the silence that followed wash over him, cracking his neck or letting his head hang down to his chest if for no other reason than to stretch the muscles in his back. The burger and fries brought him back around to reality complete with another hangry rumble of his stomach and salivating mouth. He dug into it with a barely mumbled thank you, not even noticing the refill on his beer until the plate was mostly empty. The bartender, whose name was Hadi, James learned, only smiled and offered conversation when James was not stuffing his face with food or chatted with the big guy who they called V. He ordered another round of fries and something called a s'mores pudding pie that was simply to die for.

"All right, so where are you from, New Guy?" V asked, shifting on his bar stool to look at James. James wiped his mouth and snorted.

"Arizona." V made a face. No one liked Arizona.

"James, Virgil; Virgil, James - we all just call him V," Hadi explained as he came through with fresh drinks and glasses of water for everyone. The drunk at the end of the bar was face down already, making Hadi pause to check for a pulse. "Still alive. You call this time, V."

"Yeah, ok," Virgil said, pulling his phone out. "S'cuse me a sec, Jimbo."

The police were called to take the poor drunkard away. It seemed to be a regular occurrence for the officers all waved to V and Hadi, and the waitress whose name James did not catch. Regular law enforcement presence, then. They did not seem wary of Hadi at all, or Virgil for that matter. So, they either didn't know, or had no reason for concern. Interesting. James flexed his hand again as he observed the comings and goings inside the bar, the relationships between the employees and customers; it all seemed so normal. However, a job was a job - for another day. Exhaustion began to take over, and the twitching in his arm was getting to a point where it would become embarrassing. As soon as he tried to get off the stool, he nearly fell back, his right leg completely seizing up. Had it not been for Hadi's quick latch onto the front of his shirt, he would have taken out the stool and anything else in his path on his way to the floor.

"Whoa," Hadi said, pulling James forward again until he could balance against the bar. "You ok?"

James nodded, felt the vertigo settle in and then shook his head out some. Pain radiated up his thigh. This was not going to be fun. Not knowing any better, Hadi only laughed.

"You had like, two beers, man. Am I gonna have to watch you?" Hadi teased.

"S'fine," he slurred. Great. "It's not... I'm not drunk. I uh... I'm ok. I just need to get home. I got it. Thanks."

"Want me to call you a cab?"

"No," James shook his head, shutting his eyes so he could focus on the words he was trying to get out and *not* stutter. "No, I'm... uhm... I'm just across the street."

Hadi gave him a look but shrugged and let go all the same. James turned to leave and fell right over. He felt like a fool. When he looked up, Hadi was beside him with Virgil on the other side. There was no mirth in Hadi's face anymore, just concern.

"Ok, you don't look ok," Hadi said, helping James

back to his feet. He couldn't put much weight on his right leg at all and his head pounded with pain now. Somehow, through semi-slurred directions and limping steps, James made it back across the street with the help of an Evolved ex-con and a potential arsonist. His stint in Chicago was starting fabulously.

"What floor?" Hadi asked.

"I got it," James insisted.

"James, what floor you on, man?" Hadi repeated, hefting James up a little so it was easier to hold him upright. The motion made James want to vomit.

"Three" James answered. Hadi nodded, helping him up the stairs with Virgil as back up. The man was too large to fit beside James and Hadi. Eventually, they made it to James' apartment, boxes and all, with Genevieve, his Labrador, waiting with wagging tail at the door. The only other thing of great importance he'd packed in the trailer was a single recliner that he'd paid some passing dude twenty bucks to help him carry in.

"All right," Hadi said, once the door was open, and the keys hung on a tack James had shoved into the wall earlier that day, batting Gen down with soft chuckles. "Someone missed you. You good?"

James nodded. Hadi did not look convinced but, blessedly, left James alone. He waited until he was sure he was alone before practically crawling to the bathroom to dig for his medication and collapsing right there on the cold tile floors. Genevieve curled up beside him, head in his lap.

Welcome to Chicago, he thought, leaning his head

back against the porcelain tub before drifting off to sleep.

~

The scathing headache that ripped through James's skull drew him from painful sleep, across the cold tile floors he slept on, and over to the even colder toilet sometime around 10:00am. He only knew that because his phone had an alarm set to remind him to take his meds at 10:00am. Getting old sucked. His stomach hated him, bringing up the wonderful burger and fries he'd enjoyed the night before. Not that that was good for him either, but neither was smoking or drinking and he did that despite arguments from his physicians, family, and friends. If he was gonna die, it wasn't going to be on salads and green juice.

His whole body ached and his right arm trembled something terrible. He growled as he leaned back against the cool wall of his bathroom, stomach finally settling. Genevieve came up to lick his face, making him grin. She was his lifeline. It took an hour or so for him to feel like a human being again. He showered, took his old-man meds, and lit up a cigarette to help calm his nerves. His eyes naturally narrowed against the smoke. The view from his window showed him the bar across the street. It looked different in the daytime, sort of grungy and run down. The door needed a new coat of paint, something he had not noticed the night before, and there was a bum asleep beneath the window on the left with his shopping cart full of random belongings piled high beside him.

His phone beeped out an R2-D2 pattern, pulling his attention to the high bar that separated the kitchen from the living room. There was a receipt turned over with two numbers on it: Hadi's and the number for the 13th Hour. Beneath the numbers read: 'I'm not far. Call if you need anything. Hope you feel better. Welcome to Chicago. - Haze'

James grinned. Whatever the A.E.C. thought about Hadi, he was *not* their arsonist. He wrestled with internal giddiness, hesitating at least twice before finally punching in the number that had been left behind. He could not muster the courage to call, so switched to text, typing in simply 'Thanks 4 last nite. - J'. He'd just convinced himself to not send it when the phone buzzed, making his thumb hit the 'send' button on accident anyway.

"Shit," he cursed then hit the Bluetooth at his ear. "Falcon. - - Yes, ma'am, I arrived just last night. Is Sparrow... - - Yes, ma'am. - - Yes, ma'am I have. I was there last night. - - Yes, ma'am. - - No, I'll find it."

He hung up with nothing else spoken, looking down at Gen who gave him the angelic look of adoration that all dogs give.

"Ready to go to work?" he said, digging her leash out of a box. Despite all the secrecy of the A.E.C., having Genevieve around helped James seem unimposing and more trusting; it let him do his job with greater ease than not having her. Somewhere she had a vest that indicated her as a service dog but she hated wearing it so James never bothered. She was more than a service dog, anyway. She was his partner in everything. He made sure to walk her before hailing a cab heading into the heart of Chicago. They pulled up to a building that looked grossly unassuming on the outside: stone face, only a handful of windows, and an iron gate around it with barbed wire at the top. So secretive.

"Fun," James commented, squinting up at the imposing building that stood out like a sore thumb amongst the grandeur of Chicago architecture.

"You look like shit."

James glanced over to the woman that spoke. Valerie was tall, nearly equal in height to James, with what he liked to call Nordic beauty. Everyone always asked if she were Swiss; she always told them to fuck off.

"Good to see you too, Val," James grinned. He gave the woman a long, tight hug. It had been some time since they had worked together, both assigned to different states after their initial partnering. Their last visit was under rather poor circumstances during Patrick's funeral. James was glad to see her joking around and tossing smiles; it was important. "How are the kids?"

"Insane," Valerie smiled. "They're going to eat my mother alive. I take it David didn't come out with you?"

"Did you really expect him to?" James shot back flatly. "Cuz I didn't. He loves the sun too much; the heat. Whatever. What's going on here?"

Valerie looked at the building with a grimace. "Welcome to A.E.C. headquarters."

They both made a face and a noise of disgust. Genevieve went so far as to bark a low growl at the building. The inside was, blessedly, much better. Pristine white walls met with equally pristine white floors. Everything was motion censored, state-of-the art, touch panel technology. James listened as Valerie brought him up to speed on the fires springing up like daisies in the spring all around Chicago. So far that year - barely into March - there had been four but the last one was the worst with no survivors.

"It's only a matter of time before there's another one. This guy is getting something out of these fires. PeaceKeepers think it's the Collector."

"Are you shitting me? The guy that eats souls for breakfast?"

"The one and only," Valerie said. The Collector was a well-known super villain of immense power. He plagued most of Europe for nearly ten years before disappearing. If he resurfaced in the States...

"What's the story?" James prodded carefully.

"He's not a fire manipulator last I checked."

"No, but we think he's using one to set the fires and reap the dead. It'd be a great cover. Better than the plagues in Prague. Easier to handle."

"Oh goodie," James intoned. For as much as he liked Hadi, he knew that money was a very powerful motivator and the Collector, reputedly, had a lot of it. He was not normally wrong about a person's character, but with the Collector in town, all bets were off. "So, tell me about your parolee."

"Virgil?" Valerie asked. She shrugged. "He's mostly harmless, but I hadn't even considered him as a potential accomplice. I hate your logical mind sometimes."

Chicago had a real problem, and James had just stepped into the hornet's nest.

05

"*At this time the authorities are asking citizens of Chicago to come forward with any information they may have regarding the fires that are being set throughout the city. The Chicago PD is working with Interpol, the A.E.C. and the FBI to track down the serial arsonist believed to be responsible for the most recent string of tragic fires. The subject is considered extremely dangerous, so please do not approach if seen. Any information is helpful...*"

Lonny Angram peered at the television screen displayed through the shop's window. It was one of the few box-screens left in existence, the quirky rabbit-ear antennas bent into a tilted V that only achieved a partially faded, grainy picture. The pawn shop showed a price tag of $1200 for the 'antique' on display.

"Antique my ass," Lonny grumbled. He chewed on a toothpick that stuck out of the left corner of his

mouth, periodically switching it from side to side. He'd
been a smoker clear up to his divorce date and then, suddenly, he just switched to toothpicks instead. The checkout
gals at the grocery store always looked at him funny when
he had five or six boxes on the belt with a single box of
Trix. They weren't just for kids, he'd tell them, and go
about his day.

People passed him, talking about the change in
weather and the hope for a decent summer. Not even deadly fires stopped that nonsense. Fliers for nights in the park,
and announcements for the end of the skating rink were
pinned to every tree and pole in town. People remained
purposely oblivious to the atrocities happening around
them. Lonny just shook his head at them. He used to have
these arguments with his wife, claiming to have lost faith
in a society that had put so many blinders on they needed
to be led by the nose or fall off the edge. In his mind, they
mostly got what they deserved. Some were innocent - kids
and the rare folks that showed true concern for their fellow
man. Maybe that was why he kept his day job instead of
going full mercenary. He thought about his new girl, the
cute little waitress that liked when he wore his uniform
when they had sex. She was innocent, her heart as big as
the Texas state she hailed from. The rest of them, though…

He continued on down the busy sidewalk. He was
neither rushed nor slow, pacing himself along with the rest
of the folks going to and fro. Things were going according
to plan and the cash deposits were hitting his mail box as
expected. The A.E.C. whores were crawling all over the
city like roaches. Even the PeaceKeepers were in town

- pretentious pricks. He would have to watch his back. Neither organization were people Lonny wanted to tangle with.

A noise akin to a screaming Wookie echoed out of his back pocket. A few people glanced at him, others giggled; most ignored him. He was no one to pay attention to. He dug his phone out of his pocket and looked at the address in the text message. A restaurant. Interesting. Well, he was not one to question when the money showed up on time.

"Where to?" the driver asked. He was Caucasian, surprisingly, and the cab smelled like too many Hawaiian scented air fresheners.

"Lockwood Restaurant," Lonny answered, settling into the vinyl seat. It bounced too much, but it was better than sitting inside of a body odor trap for the next fifteen minutes. He paid the guy and stood in front of the restaurant for a moment. It was a nice place, swanky; one of those yuppie places that claimed to serve all organic tofu shit or something. It connected to the Palmer House Hilton. Now it made sense.

Lonny walked in, curling his nose at the corner a bit with the scents that struck him. Definitely a yuppie place. He glanced at his phone again to read the time: 5:47pm. He had time for dinner.

"Just one this evening, sir?" the host asked. He was a young guy, probably college in the liberal arts program.

"Yeah," Lonny answered. "Bar is fine."

He was led back to the bar. There were the regular

stiffs that held their business meetings at the high tables
with tumblers of gin or old fashions in hand. Forks clinked
against plates as they cut into premium pieces of salmon
or thick, juicy cuts of steak that probably cost forty dollars
a plate. He ordered one of those with the tiny potatoes
roasted in herbs and pink salt from the Himalayas or something like that. It was the best dinner he'd had to date. He
even ate the green beans that weren't all green. Heirloom,
the menu said. Fancy that. Was a shame he had to burn it
down; Lindsay-Rae would have liked it there.

As soon as the bill was set down, Lonny wiped
his mouth, finished off his glass of top-shelf bourbon and
touched the billfold until the leather began to bubble and
boil. The heat of it transferred to the bar, making the polished wood pop and crack like a fireplace until the entire
thing ignited in a gush of flame that sped across the top
like a race car along the tracks. People screamed, falling
out of their chairs to get away from the bar. They didn't get
far. The fire spread fast; too fast. Lonny merely watched,
the only calm person in the entire place. He shook his head
at the state of things, calmly locking the doors and turning
off the fire alarms.

"Sheep," he said under his breath.

Anyone that got close to the fire ended up wrapped
in a blanket of flame that would not be put out no matter
how hard they tried. He heard the pop of cracking glass
that would hold the flames inside for at least a good thirty
minutes; long enough, he thought. He walked out through
the kitchens, the stoves and ovens exploding as he passed
them.

Outside, in the dim glow piercing through the heavy curtains and tinted doors stood a hooded figure. The guy never showed his face and used a voice modulator when he spoke. It was none of Lonny's business why, but it was a little odd.

"Well done, Mr. Angram," the figure said. He watched with sick fascination as blueish-white streaks zipped, one by one, to the figure's hands. He stood with them splayed out to the side, breathing in deep whatever the little streaks were. Lonny never asked. That's not what he was paid for. He waited, ten, fifteen minutes then jogged around the building to circle the block, pulling his phone out.

"911 Dispatch, what's your emergency?"

"Dispatch, this is Lieutenant Lonny Angram, there's a fire brewing inside the Palmer House Hilton, units are requested immediately…"

~

Pungent smoke filled the small apartment Hadi shared with his brother. It swirled in chaotic patterns above his head and rolled across the ceiling, licking its way down the walls and out the window he'd cracked open so his neighbor wouldn't pitch a fit over the stench that she swore seeped through the thin walls. Hadi shut his eyes as he exhaled a long stream of gray into the air. His muscles all felt like Jello and his head swam in a peaceful haze of zero fucks. A pile of books as tall as his bed sat beside him, his arm draped across them as if he laid back on a horizontal throne. The TV in his room ran through re-runs of *Scooby Doo* that neither held his attention nor distracted him. It simply existed as background noise to his muddled thoughts.

The rest of his room was simple, stacked floor to ceiling with bookshelves overflowing with knowledge and fictional worlds near and far. Even his dresser had books with the tiniest space reserved for a framed picture of his parents and baby sister standing in front of the Eiffel Tower. Amir studied the world around him, Hadi absorbed it. Every book he could quote nearly verbatim, their pages as familiar to him as a close lover.

He lived simply, wanted for very little, and let his mind wander through the drug-induced haze that helped him relieve the anxiety that continually crept in around him. The only distraction was the honking noise his phone made as a text message came through. Hadi pawed at his bed for the phone until feeling it hit his palm. He took another drag off his joint, squinting as he read the message:

GREG IS 4 IN 2NITE; UR GONNA LOSE. AGAIN. COME DOWN. WE'RE PLAYING DARTS. UR MISSED. - A

Hadi chuckled, dropping the phone to his belly.

The one night Hadi had off, Amir decided that books were the devil's spawn and gave up on studying. He went down to the bar to pilfer drinks and onion rings with Virgil or flirt with Lindy. She had a boyfriend now, but it was Lindy; the woman flirted with everyone, and it was as close to a woman as Amir would ever get. The kid was *terrible* with women. They shared a unique bond, Hadi and Amir. No judgment, no real expectations except to do the dishes on assigned nights or pay the few bills they had on time. They were so close in age that Lindy called them 'Texas twins'. Virgil argued that the phrase was 'Irish twins' but the meaning was still understood. So, even on his night off, Hadi made his way back to the bar he called his second home to go throw a few darts with his brother. With luck, James would be there. He liked the private investigator from Arizona. The story was told over and over at the bar, this gumshoe chasing criminals through the corrupt underbellies of big business. It was sort of romantic.

With a heavy sigh and one last drag, Hadi got himself up, shuffling out of his apartment while twisting himself into his light coat. Living above the bar made things much easier, though he still had to go through the side alley to get to the front door of the bar. The side door to the bar did not have a handle on the alley's side so there was no way in, only out. The night was cool and windy, whipping Hadi's semi-long hair into his face. He needed a trim but was too lazy to bother with it, and the longer length suited him. It was not nearly as long as Amir's - the only plus that his father saw in Hadi compared to Amir.

He put the thought out of his mind, stuffing his hands into his pockets as he trotted around the corner of the building to the 13th Hour. It was quiet, all things considered. The tiny bell above the door jingled, and that was the only warning Hadi got. A gunshot went off with such volume and force that Hadi dropped to the ground out of instinct as the door splintered right where his head had been mere moments before.

"HADI!" Amir shouted only to have the butt of a pistol slammed into his nose.

"Hey, asshole, pick on someone your own size!" Moose snarled, though there was little he could do about the situation unfolding inside the bar.

There were never any patrons on Monday evenings, except Greg who was unconscious on the floor with a giant goose egg forming on his temple, and Virgil who looked ready to chew stones. Three men in black with stereotypical ski masks over their faces held guns to the hostages, while a fourth man stuffed all the cash in the register and bar safe into a gray duffle bag.

"Bad timing, buddy," a fifth said as Hadi was hauled to his feet, gun pressed to his head. All he could do was put his hands up, as if doing so would prevent the bullet from barreling right through his skull to the other side of the bar if the gun discharged.

He looked at the others, the fear in their eyes, the concern, the rage in Virgil's eyes, the blood streaming from Amir's bruised nose. The television ran through the newscast from earlier, warning Chicago citizens of the arsonist setting fires all over the city.

"Lock it up!" one of the masked men barked. He tossed the keys to the man holding a gun to Hadi's head. He forced Hadi to lock the front doors so that there would be no more interruptions, then shoved him back to his knees with the barrel of the gun pressed to the back of his head. Hadi's stomach knotted, palms sweating, and heart thrumming so loudly in his ears it was deafening. And, of course, he felt the heat building in his core.

"Where's the other safe, lady?" the leader barked, aiming his pistol at Lindy's face. She shrank back away from him, tears making big black streaks of wet mascara down her cheeks.

"We don't got one," Lindy sobbed.

"Don't lie to me, bitch!" the man continued, pressing the barrel of the gun right to her forehead. She shrieked, shutting her eyes and shaking.

"She ain't lyin'!" Moose interjected, earning him a bullet through the shoulder that had all of them screaming. Hadi moved first, his gut reaction to go to his friend, to help him somehow. But the man that held him refused to let go, hauling him back until Hadi's head connected with the wall. His vision tunneled for a moment before unadulterated fear took over. He felt it, the fire that burned inside of him, the fire that he tried to keep in check, boiling to the surface.

Everything became reactive at that point. His head connected with the wall so his fist connected with the man's face - while on fire.

The flames created a hole in the mask and ignited the rest of it in licks of orange and blue as the flames took over Hadi's entire person. Suddenly all the guns were pointed at him, but not a single one fired. Instead, they all melted, burning the robbers' hands. They howled in pain or writhed on the floor as the heat spread from a burning sensation to actual flame. Virgil jumped in at that point, slamming two of them down onto the floor just with his shoulder. They collapsed in a boneless heap. The two still writhing inside of Hadi's fire trap howled, creating such a ruckus that Hadi snarled. He wrapped them all up in a tornado of flame that sent them crashing through the front door in an explosion of wood and ash right onto the street. Only one of them moved, running in a lurch while scream- ing about the man on fire.

Hadi got a good look at himself in the reflection of the bar and stopped short. His eyes burned like coals, hair a whiplash of flames and skin that appeared like cooling lava. In a matter of seconds, he shut his power down, feel- ing the cool blast of the coming spring whip back through the busted door as he sagged and stumbled. No one moved. The entire bar now smelled vaguely of smoke and ashes or urine. The walls around the broken door had black streaks of soot and tiny bubbles in the wood from the high tem- peratures that struck them. Hadi felt his heart sink. Moose leaned heavily against the liquor shelves with one hand over his shoulder. Blood seeped out between his fingers as he stared wide-eyed at Hadi; at a pyro freak that just lost his shit in front of everyone.

Hadi stared back at them, feeling the bile rise in his throat and his stomach twist into nauseating knots. He knew he should probably bolt before the cops came or those Men in Black freaks so hell-bent on digging through his life's story just to be pricks. Instead, he stood there with his mouth gaping, slowly backing away towards the door like a frightened dog.

"God, Hadi," Lindy breathed out, tears still streaming down her face. She moved from behind the bar so suddenly that Hadi was completely caught off guard when her arms wrapped themselves tightly around his neck. "Thank you."

Hadi froze. He couldn't even wrap his arms

around Lindy to return the gesture; shock prevented his limbs from moving. She sobbed into his shoulder, repeating 'thank you, thank you' over and over again.

"Wow, man… Think we might need to change your name to Hellfire…" Moose finally breathed out. Hadi looked up at him. Amir stood beside him with a rag pressed to the giant man's shoulder now and a couple napkins stuffed into his own nose. His little brother just smiled proudly at him. Virgil smirked, shaking his head knowingly.

"No one says nothin', hear?" Lindy said suddenly, half turning while still half holding to Hadi's shoulder. "Nothin' happened."

"Lindy, honey, he blew the door off its hinges. There's not much that'll hide *that*," Virgil said.

"And you just crushed two of 'em with your pinky!" Lindy hollered back. "I swear by Jesus and my slutty stilettos I will beat y'all stupid if you breathe a word! Make.It.Up!"

The men all blinked at her, more terrified of her threat than of Hadi, when they heard a groan from the floor.

"Did I faint?" Greg mumbled, rubbing the goose egg on his head. It broke the tension, allowing everyone to move a little more freely to chairs or to help Greg as the lights of the police cars began to flash in blue and red outside the blown door.

06

James jogged through the Chicago police department towards the holding cells with Genevieve trotting along behind him in a bright pink vest that made her floppy ears droop. Four A.E.C. agents spoke with the officers, Angelo 'Duck' Gustavo among them, with his Ray-Bans on despite the late hour and incredible *lack* of sunlight. James had not expected to see them, shot them a warning look to keep their traps shut, and continued on behind the officer that brought him in. Duck glared, but blessedly kept his mouth shut; for now.

"We don't normally listen to federal folks," the officer explained. He was one of the few that graced the bar regularly to collect Greg; James could not recall his name. "We've got our own branch here in Chicago that work well with us so the *real* feds tend to put us out a bit. But they were stupid insistent that we bring Haze down. I don't know what for; poor guy nearly wet himself with what happened at that bar tonight."

"What happened? He.. He didn't tell me anything, just said he needed bail," James said. Which was true. And, the officer was not wrong. Hadi sounded like he might vomit over the phone, voice shaking and weak.

"Yeah, I don't like that either. That asshole in the Ray-Bans said the kid wasn't allowed to go unless someone paid his bail which puts him on the watch list - ours and theirs. It's stupid. You go to the bar, don't you? I've seen you."

"Yeah... yeah, I owe Hadi a favor," James lied.

He, honestly, didn't know *why* Hadi thought to call *James* for bail, but considering the mess downtown at the Hilton and the rumors he was hearing from the bar, he was glad of it. "So, what happened?"

"Bar got robbed. They shot Moose and messed up Hadi's kid brother pretty bad. Feds made us arrest Virgil too. His parole officer already came to get him. She yelled at them something fierce though for bringing him in."

"The bar got *robbed*?"

"Yeah. Assholes tried to set the place on fire too. Guess Virgil shoved them all through the front door. They pulled him in on aggravated assault, of all things. Poor staff probably wouldn't be alive if he hadn't been so aggravated. Feds won't tell me what the charges are on Hadi. Poor kid's scared shitless. I gave him some coffee but I think that made it worse. He's over here."

The holding cells were like anything James might expect: dull, gray, small, and smelly. While everyone else at the bar had been taken to the hospital, the two Evolved had been arrested on A.E.C. orders. James shook his head, glancing back over in the direction he knew Duck and his flock of worshipers to be.

Way to keep it on the down low, guys, he thought. If that guy messed up his stake-out, he was going to turn that thick-browed idiot into a pretzel.

Hadi looked awful. He sagged on the metal bench bolted to the wall, hands still in cuffs. In fact, he looked green if James had to put a color to him. He learned why, too, as the poor bartender suddenly sagged forward and fell off the bench.

"Haze!" James called. Both he and the officer - who still had no name in James's mind - rushed to the cell, unlocking the barred door. Gen barked, whining and pawing at the door like when she knew someone to be in distress. He hadn't even had time to take her home before Hadi called, following along with her little vest sliding off her back. "Haze? Hey? Hadi?"

His pulse was weak, and he felt clammy to the touch. James gave him a good look over, finding crusted blood on the back of his neck.

"Did he get checked out by medical before being brought in?" James demanded. The officer shook his head. Gen licked a scar on Hadi's right palm.

"No, they wouldn't let it happen, they just dragged him and Virgil in here."

James let his fingers run through Hadi's hair until finding what he sought: a gash on the back of his head with a large enough bump to give him all the information he needed.

"He's got a head wound, probably a concussion. Hadi? Haze? Hey, look at me, come on, kiddo - call the ambulance, I don't give a flying fuck what those assholes in suits say."

The officer nodded. James stayed with Hadi all the way to the hospital, planting himself beside the bed, Genevieve at his feet. It was not a bad concussion, but still required a hospital stay and some stitches to close the head wound. James made three calls to headquarters and two to Valerie to get all the details and figure out what moron sent Angelo Gustavo to handle the incident at the bar. There were too many details missing. It was Hadi's night off, thus, it was sort of James's night off.

He'd gone to Valerie's for dinner then out to catch a movie when he'd received Hadi's call plus five messages from headquarters about the fire at the Hilton. It was a giant cluster.

"James?"

He looked up to find Amir standing in the door with a bandage on his now-broken nose. Both eyes were bruised as a result, and he had a butterfly bandage on his cheek. James was not as familiar with Hadi's brother as he was with Hadi, having only talked to the kid twice at best. They looked alike, close in age and height.

"Hey, Amir - you ok?" James asked, rising to his feet with a twist of his stiff shoulders. Genevieve shifted but did not rise, content to stay where she was. Amir nodded, glancing at his brother with worry.

"What happened?" he asked. "The cops, they took him like he did something wrong but he was fine when -"

"He's ok," James cut in. "Minor head wound and a concussion. Did the guys robbing you hit him or something?"

Amir shook his head. "They shoved him against the wall pretty hard; tried messing with him. Why is this happening, James? Hadi didn't do nothing to nobody. They almost killed him!"

"I don't know, Amir," James sighed, sitting back down. He reached down to pet Gen, letting his stress wash away with her presence. "I want to help him, Amir, but you gotta be straight with me, ok?"

Amir nodded. James gestured for him to shut the sliding door and take a seat. When things were quiet, James continued.

"Amir, is your brother Evolved?"

The look of surprise on Amir's face would have been confirmation enough, but the eventual reluctant nod solidified it.

"What are his powers?"

Amir hesitated, glancing at Hadi as if debating between helping his brother and keeping his secret. "Fire. He didn't do anything wrong. They've been harassing him since I got here."

"How many guys robbed you, Amir?" James asked. He read the report. Valerie sent it to him shortly after collecting Virgil. She was livid. The arrest put Virgil's probation at risk and took a key witness away from one of their suspects; a suspect that was now in a hospital bed with a nasty concussion.

"Five," Amir answered without looking up. The

report had only two of them arrested, all taken to the hospital for burns or broken bones.

"Amir, they only arrested two of them."

"So? The others ran or something," Amir argued. His voice quavered and cracked a little. James took in a calming breath.

"Amir, I can't help him if you're not honest with me."

"One of them ran," Amir finally relented, looking at his brother. He didn't say anything else. No bodies had been recovered and there would not have been enough time to 'hide' evidence. All the police found were splintered pieces of wood, some of the pieces burned, and very frightened victims. If only one of them ran...

"Good lord," James sighed, pressing the bridge of his nose between both hands.

"James?" Hadi croaked, making James's head snap up. Hadi stirred, trying to look around at the small room with little success.

"Hey," James said, rising to his feet again. The confusion on Hadi's face suddenly turned to panic, making him groan and roll to a near sitting. "Hey, hey, you're fine. It's ok. You're in a hospital. You've got a concussion."

"Am—" Hadi tried, breathing hard with a wild look in his eyes.

"He's fine. Everyone's ok. Amir's right here. Re-lax. Ok? You're fine. I even brought Gen to see you."

James gave a short whistle, and the dog hopped up onto the bed. Hadi grinned, relaxing instantly beneath her weight. She was as much a regular to the bar as James or Greg, or the guy that ordered the fish sandwiches on Friday nights. Everyone loved her, Hadi included. He put his hand on her head, smiling more when she licked his palm, shutting his eyes again. James glanced over at Amir and shook his head.

"Amir."

The new voice drew James' attention to the glass door. An older man with similar features to Amir and Hadi stood with his hand holding the door open.

"Saleh," Amir said, moving to the older man; their cousin. Hadi's dossier was surprisingly detailed. The elder man owned a laundromat, was newly married, and had an infant daughter. He also took Amir into a tight embrace while glaring at James.

Overly protective too, it would seem.

They spoke in Arabic under the assumption that James was just another ignorant white man. He let them think that, sitting slowly with a heavy sigh. Saleh urged Amir to go back home, or move in with him, but *not* to get involved with the mess Hadi had made for himself. Amir argued against it, refusing to abandon his brother 'the way everyone else had'. Part of James was glad for Amir's unwavering support, part of him wanted to tell Amir to run for the hills like his cousin. This was only going to get worse before it got better; so much worse.

~

Zephyr glared at the group of A.E.C. agents clustered together in the searing white conference room on the third floor of Chicago headquarters. They were all, every single one of them, complete idiots.

"One hotel fire," she said slowly, walking among them with piercing eyes. "And a robbery where things *almost* went up in a wild conflagration of *fuck ups!* Are any of you capable of actually doing your job!"

"Ma'am, if I may-"

"Shut up, Angelo!" Zephyr barked, using the man's actual name and glaring with unadulterated fury. He wore his stupid sunglasses like he always did, hiding behind them as he dropped his chin to his chest in castigation. "If, *if* that bartender is at all involved your complete *idiocy* may have wiped it completely from his memory. Arrest does not preclude one from medical attention, you dimwit! I ought to have Ronin drop you into a shadow for the next month!"

To his credit, Duck swallowed hard and looked down at his feet.

"Sparrow!" Zephyr continued. Valerie stepped forward. "Falcon!"

James did the same, Genevieve trotting along beside him with a straight back and perky ears. She'd found a way to remove her vest, sitting proudly with just her glossy brown coat and pink collar.

"You two seem to be the only competent agents in the Chicago field office," Zephyr continued. "I'm placing you both on point. I want to know everything about the bartender, Falcon, down to how often he shits. If we're wasting efforts on him, I need to know now so we can redirect our attention elsewhere. Are we even certain he's Evolved?"

"We are, ma'am," Falcon answered in the affirmative. "Fire manipulation, unfortunately."

"You have an opinion already, Agent Falcon?" Zephyr pressed, stepping closer to the man with the scruffy beard and too-long hair. He was taller than she, but that was not difficult for her; she was a very petite woman.

"Partial, ma'am," Falcon said while staring at a fixed point away from Zephyr's face. Military trained, indeed.

"Do share, I don't have the patience to tiptoe through bullshit."

Now he looked at her. She knew she was not the easiest person to stomach. She cursed like a sailor and threw her money around like it was a helium balloon, but she also lead the PeaceKeepers with thorough knowledge and well-proven tactics. She treated the agents beneath her the same and expected results, results she was not getting. Already there were whispers all over Chicago about 'the Evolved freaks' and the cops sent in to hunt them down. *Hunt them down.* Those were not words she wanted to hear among the populace. They created a panic and high sense of paranoia that made her job harder.

"His power is reactive, ma'am," Falcon explained. "There is a past trauma that feeds into it, I think. PTSD that's never been treated. I don't believe he is consciously capable of committing the types of crimes we're seeing. He would have to be hard-pressed to do it, something to trigger that anxiety response and keep it fueled until it's finished."

"So noted," Zephyr said, stepping a little closer. "Make sure he isn't triggered. White on rice, Agent Falcon, by any means necessary. Understood?"

"Yes, ma'am."

"Agent Sparrow, set your hound to hunt," Zephyr continued. "That man knows people who know more people. I want to know those people; I want to know the fleas on their back. Dig. Bargain his parole sentence if you have to."

"Is that wise, ma'am. He's a convicted super-villain," Duck interrupted. Zephyr narrowed her eyes at him as if doing so would burn a hole right through his skull to the lack of a brain he seemed to posses.

"Do super-villain's have friends and play with service dogs specifically trained to maul people like him, Agent *Gustavo*?" Angelo had no answer, blubbering like the fool he was, verbally demoted in a room full of his peers and betters. "Kindly shut the fuck up. You will all canvas the Chicago area for *anything* that even *smells* of arson or unusual death. All the hobos in an alley suddenly pass from exposure, I need to know about it. You will report directly to Agent Sparrow or Agent Falcon who will both report directly to me. I do not have the patience to deal with the ass-hattery of this branch. Dismissed."

James left A.E.C. headquarters with a grimace on his face. 'Any means necessary' was a rather broad term and not something James particularly cared for. He liked Hadi; probably liked him a little *too* much. Gen walked beside him, periodically looking up at him with worry in her big brown eyes. She felt his stress, the tension in his muscles that he had to be wary of. Medicines only went so far. Stress made his condition worse which, in turn, stressed him out even more.

Zephyr had a point, however. If there was something wrong with Hadi *or* Virgil, she'd have torn them to pieces by now. The only one she didn't really like was Duck, but that wasn't hard. No one liked Duck. Still, he looked to his four-legged partner for wisdom but only saw big brown eyes with no clear answers.

"I cannot believe I'm doing this, Gen," he said, pulling his phone out as he stormed through Millennium Park. Headquarters was not far. If there were more windows, the view would be phenomenal.

As it was, he got to look at antiseptic white walls and clear touch panels any time he was in that horrid building. He scrolled through the contacts until finding Hadi's number. The bartender was on leave following his head injury, the bar closed for a few days to do repairs. No one really wanted to be inside the bar after what happened anyway. James couldn't blame them.

Trauma of any kind was a very powerful thing. He'd read Hadi's file, read about the hate crime that left him in the hospital for three months and another young man dead. James didn't even want to imagine what that was like. He was very careful with his privacy, his life, his partners for reasons just like what Hadi endured. What made it worse, were the reports starting to circulate about people being lynched or beaten by friends and neighbors, people they trusted, under suspicion of being Evolved. So far, the A.E.C. wasn't doing a good job at maintaining their secrets.

"Hey, it's James," he said into the phone as he

slowed his steps near the Bean. "Feeling better?- - Good. -
- No, no worries. I'm glad you called me.- - Listen, uhm…
the bar is closed but I still need to eat dinner. How 'bout
I cook for you for a change? - - Ok, fair. Moose normally
cooks for me. No offense to Moose, though, I don't wanna
cook *him* dinner. - - Yeah, tonight. You up for it or… - -
Ok. Seven? - - See you then. - - Bye."

James pressed the Bluetooth, then proceeded to
smack himself with his phone.

"I'm going to regret this…" he said to Gen, whistling for her to follow as he continued on past the Bean to
hail a cab.

~

Hadi laughed at James's misfortune as a child.
Somehow, falling face-first into mud in front of everyone
was funny to everyone *but* James. Still, it was a tidbit of
information that bred trust, a story of vulnerability. The
wine helped. Dating was not really James's thing. His last
partner had courted him, and was not related to work in
any capacity. Just a nice guy at a bar. This just felt awkward. All the same, he made a good show of it, cooking his
famous veal Parmesan and, even went so far as to shave
most of his beard off so he didn't look so awfully rugged,
and a little more… polished, Valerie would call it. Despite
orders and awkwardness, James genuinely enjoyed Hadi's
company. Secretly, he wished for this date to be the real
deal, to be casual and innocent rather than something he
needed to do for work.

"You must have been cute as a kid," Hadi grinned.
James snorted. He was a terror as a kid, but that was beside

the point. His mother kept decent enough pictures that now sat in a box under his bed; he'd been cute enough.

"Not as cute as you, I'd wager," James said without thinking, refilling the wine glasses. Hadi smirked at him. "What?"

"Nothing," Hadi smiled. "So, why Genevieve?"

"Why'd I get her, or why'd I name her that?"

James asked, handing Hadi his refilled glass of wine. Gen wagged her tail at the sound of her name, looking up from the sofa. Hadi looked at her and smiled.

"Why'd you name her that? Why you got her is sorta obvious," Hadi shrugged. Gen went almost everywhere with James. He did not hide his condition from anyone; there was no point. Most people stared, wondering if he really *needed* a service dog. He didn't *look* sick; not usually. Hadi never questioned it or thought it out of the ordinary either.

"She is the patron saint of Paris," James explained. "I was stationed in France for three years. Paris is one of my favorite cities. Besides, she's *my* saint, right, Gen?"

The dog barked, making both men laugh. Small talk was not going to get James the answers he needed, however. He needed to up his game.

"So... what's with you and Lindy?" James asked. It was a curiosity of his and potentially useful information. He observed how the two interacted and heard mention of their relationship. They were close. It was really none of James's business, but orders from on high made it his business. Hadi only shrugged.

"Nothing, really. Just friends," Hadi answered,

sipping the wine. "She's got a boyfriend. Fireman, I think. Seems nice. He treats her good."

"A fireman? Like, a firefighter?"

"Yeah. It's been freaking her out there's so much fire lately. She worries about him. He's been at most of the bad fires. I guess they're kinda serious. She keeps talking about taking him back to Texas."

"But you still cash in on some benefits?" James pressed. Hadi grinned.

"Does that bother you, Detective Kendall?" Hadi smirked. James grinned back, feeling like an ass for lying to Hadi. His cover was as a private investigator looking into a large firm in Chicago. The story was told almost nightly because the bar miscreants, as James liked to call them, liked to live vicariously through James. Lindy had even called it romantic, one time; Hadi agreed.

Even Virgil remained clueless thanks to Valerie's quick wit and explanations when he was seen with her. James wanted so badly to tell Hadi the truth. Given the kid's past experiences with the A.E.C., however, that would be the worst idea in the history of bad ideas, especially now. Instead, he leaned in a little closer and smiled.

"No," James said, daring to be bold. He kissed Hadi, ignoring the screaming morality jumping up and down at the back of his head. He needed Hadi to open up, to trust him with more than a request for bail. The wine most definitely helped.

Every footstep Lonny took echoed back at him in triplicate. It was an odd thing, something born of the exposed metal beams and siding in the warehouse the Contractor always insisted on meeting in. It all seemed horribly cliche to Lonny: secretive dude with a penchant for dark, mysterious, and often creepy places. Whatever, so long as the money showed up in his mailbox, he wasn't going to be judge and jury on someone else's style. He took his time, in no rush to hear the newest complaint his most recent employer had. The Contractor was a very specific individual in addition to being a little on the dark and creepy. Things had to be done exactly to the letter, or they became very irate very quickly.

"You're late," came the unnaturally disturbing voice. It was too deep, too gravelly, too mechanical. Lonny wanted to equate it to one of the voice changing toys his kid used to have, but the tonality was more natural than those cheap pieces of shit.

"Traffic," Lonny replied as he came to a stop several feet away from the mysterious Contractor. Trust was not something easily given in Lonny's world, most especially to creeps that didn't like showing their faces. Then, there was Ray-Bans. Lonny never saw the man's eyes, but he always wore black, like the Contractor, and Ray-Ban sunglasses. He stood just to the left of the Contractor like some weird body guard. It was comical, after a fashion.

"We have new information and a growing problem," the Contractor continued. Lonny sighed, cracked his neck and stuffed his hands into his pockets lest he become even more agitated than he already was. The A.E.C. was a *huge* problem; people were talking. "It is time to move on and redirect attention elsewhere, Mr. Angram. There is a second pyro that the A.E.C. are investigating. A bartender. Make sure they keep looking in that direction."

"A bartender?" Lonny said.

"Works at the 13th Hour," Ray-Bans said. "Fire manipulator. History of trauma. Little brother and familial relationship with his co-workers. The A.E.C. is watching him, but new information is pulling the attention away from him. They're going to drop him like a bad habit. He's volatile; uncontrolled power that can light up all of Chicago."

"So… you want that I should trigger him or something?" Lonny asked uncertainly. Lindsay-Rae worked at that bar. His little bubble of sunshine. This was now hitting a little too close to home for his liking.

"I want you to do your job, Mr. Angram," the Contractor said calmly. "Make it convincing; dramatic."

Lonny tilted his head and frowned. This was not in his contract. While he had no problems carrying out his requested tasks, roughing up some kid just because *they* couldn't stand the heat coming down on them was not in Lonny's job description. The kid, like Lindsay-Rae, was an innocent. His life was already being made miserable if the A.E.C. was looking in his direction. What more did the Contractor want? All of Chicago in an ash pit?

"Is there a problem, Mr. Angram?" the Contractor said.

"You're basically asking me to set off a nuclear explosion in East Side Chicago…"

"Just do your job, Angram," Ray-Bans snarled. "The kid needs to be handled! So does the A.E.C.!"

Lonny's eyes narrowed, the pupils beginning to glow like embers as his temper rose. He took a single step towards the man in the Ray-Bans, leaning in ever so slightly.

"Don't threaten me, asshole," Lonny growled. "The cops in the city are running like headless chickens because of me. They've got no real back-up, thanks to me, or did you forget that little bit? That was done without pay-ment, I might add, because you dumb asses didn't do your proper homework. You would not have this kind of free-dom if I hadn't torched Venganza like a fucking Christmas roast!"

One of the few openly accepted Evolved in the city, Venganza, *was* Chicago's primary defense. When Lonny was contracted four years prior, the vigilante got dangerously close to learning the truth, so quickly became the next victim. His wife and kids had burned too. Lonny didn't feel too good about that, even now, but sometimes shit happened. Sometimes, it happened too much.

The Contractor took a step forward, revealing just enough for Lonny to back down. The hood they wore was deep, hiding facial features but for the eyes - ice blue, frozen, emotionless and deadly.

"Trigger the bartender, Mr. Angram, by any means you see fit," the Contractor said. "You will be well compensated. We will redirect the A.E.C."

Lonny swallowed hard on the lump that grew in his throat and simply nodded.

"Most excellent," the Contractor said, taking a step back into the shadows. They then handed Lonny a manilla envelope, fat with cash he was not expecting. "Your new target. No survivors, Mr. Angram. Too many complications arise when there are survivors."

Lonny looked at the envelope, then back up at the Contractor and his crony. He tucked the envelope beneath his left arm and merely sighed, turning on his heel. He needed to be out of that weird warehouse, away from the Contractor. He needed a new job, a new life.

Maybe Lindsay-Rae might fancy a move to California. Lonny always liked it there. Chicago was getting too tense for his liking.

~

Much like most mornings for James, the sunlight brought with it a scathing headache and a need to move lest he become a permanent part of his very large bed. He

cracked his neck, rolled his shoulder and carefully slid out
from beneath Hadi's sleeping form. Gen slept at the foot of
the bed, comfortably nestled on top of the pile of discard-
ed clothes. She glanced up at him as he shuffled to the
bathroom, shaking herself out and wagging her tail at him
when he came back out. He smiled down at her, throwing on a pair of sweatpants as he made his way out to the
kitchen where his row of meds awaited. He glared at them,
hating the need for them, but began popping all their tops
all the same.

The phone he left out on the counter rattled, buzzing and singing a crazy Cantina diddy. James practically
fell over trying to get to it before the ringtone woke Hadi.
He cleared his throat, sliding the button over and placing
the flat phone to his ear since his Bluetooth was nowhere
in sight.

"Falcon," he said, brushing his hair back from his
brow. "Val? - - No, no, slow down, *what* just happened? - -
Yes, I had eyes on him all night. White on rice, I believe,
was the order given. - - *All* of them??- - No, I'm leaving
now. Lemme get a shirt. - - Because you woke me up,
dammit! It's like… like… nine. - - Yeah, I'll see you in
five."

He ended the call, tossing the phone onto the sofa.
As he turned to go back into the bedroom he jumped,
feeling his heart lurch up into his throat. Hadi stood in the
doorway, arms folded, but blessedly in boxers or it would
have made things much more awkward.

"Jesus Christ, Haze…" James breathed out. "Look,
I'm not normally one to cut and run but something's come

up with my client."

He explained as he dug through the pile for a shirt and a pair of socks. Somewhere he had a pair of shoes, hopping around like an idiot until he was dressed.

"It's ok," Hadi chortled.

"It isn't," James sighed, truly meaning it. The night before had been surprisingly pleasant and genuinely informative. "I'm really sorry. I feel like an ass."

"It's fine, really," Hadi said with more understanding and compassion in those three words than James had heard in his entire life. He meant what he said. James paused, looking at this young man, this *kid* nearly half his age and melted. The night before meant more than just gaining information, James felt it in his chest, in the butterflies that took flight in his stomach. He walked over to Hadi, reaching up to press his brow to the slightly taller young man's.

"I owe you waffles, handsome," James said softly, giving Hadi a quick kiss before bolting out the door, whistling for Gen to follow. "Lock up behind you, please! See you tonight!"

It took almost thirty minutes to get across town.

The chaos was tangible. Fire trucks and ambulances filled a narrow street. The metro bridge that sat above rows of small homes was a charred, mangled mess, half of it dangling off the tracks. Five houses were burned, nothing left but cinders. People in pajamas and sweats hovered about, some with soot on their faces. Several were laid out on stretchers or sitting on the curb where it was not flooded from the hydrants that had been used to put out the fire. James glanced around, looking for Valerie or Zephyr. He found Valerie first.

"How many?" James asked.

"Fifteen agents," Valerie sighed. "They were all on their way in to work. The fire spread to the homes when the train blew off the track."

"Jesus Christ…" James breathed out. His arm twitched, reminding him how quickly he'd left his apartment. He bit down on his lower lip and squeezed his hand into a fist until his nails bit into his palm. He did not have time for an episode.

"Are you *sure* you had eyes on your guy all night?" Valerie asked. He could hear the doubt in her voice, the *need* to blame someone for the loss of so many of their own.

"Val, I swear. I was with him all night," he said, biting his tongue too late. Valerie looked at him, then rolled her eyes.

"James Edmond Kendall…" she began.

"Don't," he warned. "You are not my mother. My orders were clear."

"That was *not* what she meant!" Valerie hissed. He was about to answer when a commotion by the blockade line took both their attention. "Shit."

"I said get outta my way!"

James knew the bellowing voice, following Valerie to the blockade. Virgil shoved his way to the front, arguing with three police officers that refused to budge. He saw Valerie and pointed at her, then saw James and frowned.

"You got family here too, Jimbo?"

"Family?" James asked, confused.

"It's fine, he's with me," Valerie said to the officers still trying to impede Virgil's forward momentum. "Your daughter's safe, Virgil. She was the first person I checked on."

"Where is she? Is she safe? Is she with her mom?" Virgil persisted, switching between staring at James and pleading with Valerie. James tried to shrink into the sopping wet grass.

"She's with her grandmother, actually. She wasn't even home. Her mom is fine too, but you can't be here right now, Virgil. This could look really bad for you."

"I don't give a shit how it looks. You said her mom was fine, is she safe?" Virgil persisted.

"Laura has minor smoke inhalation," Valerie explained. "She got out before the fire got too bad. She'll be fine. I've got armed agents on her to be sure."

"My ass! We might not get on anymore, but that's my baby's momma. She needs her mom, not promises to keep them safe! Your agents can't do shit that don't come out of a paper bag! You give Detective Kendall the same spiel?"

"Detec- -" Valerie said before catching herself. "Virgil, you need to go home. I'll check in later."

"I'll drive you home, V," James offered. "They won't let me check in either."

"I ain't goin' nowhere," Virgil stated, folding his arms and planting his large posterior on the hood of someone's car. The poor car groaned under Virgil's weight, indenting on the top to match Virgil's outline.

"If, uh.. If anything changes, Agent, please give me a call," James said. He needed to leave before things got worse. Except, they got worse.

"Agent Falcon!"

James flinched. Virgil looked right at him and frowned.

"Agent?" he asked. James wanted to crawl under a rock. "Falcon? What is this?"

"Please tell me you had eyes on your man during this debacle," Zephyr pressed. Her eyes were pools of barely contained rage. Four others of her team followed, only some that James could name. Despite being internationally known, the PeaceKeepers did their best to stay out of the public eye with few exceptions. Zephyr was one of them, but she was their leader.

Neurophage was another that James was familiar with - a mega genius that openly worked with the likes of Elon Musk, NASA, and Interpol; Ronin who was always with Zephyr. The other two were unfamiliar to him - an elderly gentleman that wore a bowler hat and refused to hide his appearance, and an Asian man who wore dark glasses and tactical gear. None of it really mattered, but having four of the PeaceKeepers stare him down made him feel worse; made his arm twitch even more.

"Yes, ma'am, I did," James finally answered, unable to move away from Virgil. "You asked for white on rice at any cost. He did not leave my sight."

Genevieve chose that point in time to bark, loudly, growling at one of the firefighters working the scene. He was an older gentleman with a thick beard. James tried to shush, Gen, but she kept at it, though she remained at James' side. He frowned at her, hissing, then looking at the man who continued on about his business. Something Hadi said the night before suddenly struck him. Lindy's boyfriend. Gen did not just bark at anyone; she barked at Evolved. The pyro was a first-responder.

"Genevieve!" James finally roared, silencing the dog. He looked at Zephyr and the rest of the PeaceKeepers with her, wracking his mind for a way to speak without being heard. "She doesn't like firemen. The hats scare her."

Zephyr was about to argue about the stupidity of such a thing. He saw it in her face, that rage that caught him up for his idiotic comment when the elder gentleman beside her suddenly caught James' eye.

It's a firefighter. The arsonist is a first responder.

"Dogs are incredibly sensitive to such things," the man said. James felt like his head had just been thrown through a washing machine. It was as if the words were yanked from his brain, swirled around, and shoved back in. It was so jarring, he staggered back and fell onto the concrete.

"James!" Valerie said. For once, he was glad of the lack of medication. It provided the perfect cover to whatever *that* was.

"I'm... f-f..." he tried, his words fading away to a stammer he did not try to stop.

"Allow me," the same man said. James tried to flinch away but stiffened instead, shutting his eyes when the man's fingers touched his temples. The jarring sensation went away, with a whispered apology that James was positive only he heard. "Better?"

Eyes still closed, James nodded, then just as quickly turned to the side and wretched. He was getting too old for this shit.

WORKED LATE. FEEL LIKE CRAP. ENJOY OPENING NIGHT W/OUT ME. SORRY, HAZE. WAFFLES NEXT TIME. BRING SOUP LATER. WE'LL TALK. - J

Hadi smiled at the text on his phone, feeling oddly giddy and euphoric. Amir had class that night but promised to stop by after for the grand re-opening. Everyone at the 13th Hour rooted for the younger Shahir, cheering him on for tests or presentations and then celebrating his triumphs with lots of booze and darts after. Hadi was glad Amir could have that kind of support. It was a shame James did not feel well, but it happened more often than not. James didn't like to admit it, but Hadi could see it in the older man's face on the days he still came for dinner and felt like crap. It would probably get too rowdy in the bar for James, anyway. The man never stayed too long in a crowd.

There were empty Corona buckets all over the bar

and at each table with a printed paper asking for donations to finish the last of the repairs and remodels. Tamara came in to collect the cash inside at the beginning of Hadi's shift and would be back to relieve him later so he could celebrate with Amir. His head still hurt a lot when he worked too long. He couldn't fall back on a quick sniff or hit while at work, so chewed aspirin instead, stuffing the bottle into his coat pocket after grabbing four little white pills.

"Hey, Haze," V said as he sat down. Hadi had not even heard the man come in. He put his phone away and frowned at the large man that had become his close friend.

"What's up, V? You ok? Want your fries?" Hadi asked. Virgil shook his head.

"Just a beer." Hadi frowned in earnest. Virgil Krisken *never* ordered 'just' a beer. He was never quiet either, always larger than life with an infectious personality that drew everyone in.

"V?" Hadi pressed, even going so far as to knock the other man in the arm. He gave a questioning head jerk, straightening briefly to get the man his requested beer. "Everything ok?"

"Yeah, yeah…" Virgil said then shook his head. "My little girl. She's sixteen. I don't hardly see her, you know. Her mom don't want me to. I get it, it's fine. Those fires, Haze… those fires were at her house."

"V…" Hadi said with great concern, sending up a quick prayer for the girl's protection.

"She's fine," Virgil said, gulping down the beer and throwing a ten in the bucket closest to him. Hadi refilled the glass without asking. "She's fine. But, too close to home, you know? I've done stupid shit. I know it. Cops know it. I'm all right with it. I made my choices but, she's just a kid, Haze. She don't need to get caught up in this."

"Can't your parole officer do something to help? Like, I dunno, protective custody or something?"

Whatever Hadi said, the look in Virgil's eyes changed from worry to near rage in a matter of seconds. He snorted and downed the second glass of beer, slamming it down on the bar.

"How was your date?"

Hadi blinked at the change of topic but let it slide, shrugging. "Fine. It was nice. He left in a hurry in the morning, though. Said he owes me waffles. Asked for soup tonight. He was gonna come for the re-opening but, I guess he's not feeling well."

"Yeah, I'll bet," Virgil scoffed. Hadi frowned. "He's duping you, Hadi."

Now Hadi let his shock show. In all the time Hadi worked at the 13th Hour and known Virgil, the man had *never* used his actual name.

"What are you talking about?"

"The guy is an Ace goon," Virgil explained.

The term had become familiar to Hadi as a slur for the A.E.C. agents that liked to lord over all the Evolved or harass innocent people from the shadows. People like Hadi and Virgil; Tam's son, apparently, as Hadi had come to learn. Virgil practically spat the single syllable in disgust.

"Christ, V, where'd you hear that shit?" Hadi laughed, refilling the glass for a third time. "He's a private investigator."

"Comes in here every night, don't he? Usually. What'd he make for dinner?" Virgil asked.

"Veal parm, why?" Hadi frowned.

"You think a guy that can make decent veal parm is gonna come eat shit bar food every night just cuz? Conveniently showed up after them Ace assholes were harassing you, didn't he? Take it from someone intimately familiar with those ass-hats - he's duping you. Ask him yourself if you don't believe me."

Hadi felt his throat clench, swallowing on a lump in his throat. He prepped the soup shortly after Amir arrived. His presence changed the mood of the bar for the better. Tam came in to relieve Hadi, smiling and cheering Amir on with everyone else. They laughed and celebrated, even cheered V up a little while Hadi collected a container of tomato soup from the kitchen and clocked out.

He walked across the street feeling like he was about to step into a dark alley. His chest hurt and he shivered despite the warmer weather. The trek up the stairs was worse. His feet were like iron weights, and his head swam with terrible scenarios. He did not want to believe Virgil, but something about the sincerity and anger in the large man's voice would not let Hadi simply dismiss what was said. He stood in front of James' door for a good ten minutes before finally knocking. Gen barked on the other side. Hadi could hear her jumping on the door and James telling her he was on his way. The latch clattered against the plywood and the door opened to a rather warm, but cozy atmosphere. The TV was on, spilling its light and sound out into the living room. The kitchen light was on and the windows open, making the blinds clang against the glass.

"Hey," James said, reaching out to give Hadi a quick peck on the cheek. "You seriously brought soup."

"You asked," Hadi shrugged. James let him in, smiling. To his credit, he looked awful, eyes sunken, and the color drained from his face a little as if he'd been fighting a fever that just broke. That was not how Hadi should be thinking, but it gave him a small sliver of hope that not *everything* was a lie.

"Don't be a stranger," James said. "Want a beer? You gotta go back?"

Hadi shook his head. "I'm good. I clocked out. We're gonna play darts with Amir. He passed his exams."

"Good for him," James said, genuinely meaning it. Hadi watched him pull out the soup, then heard the buzz of James' phone. He watched James pick it up, reading the message that came through and frown.

"Everything ok, Agent Kendall?" Hadi asked casually. He pet Gen on the head when she came to him. He held no animosity towards the dog.

"Yeah, just a work… thing…" James said, suddenly realizing what he'd answered to. Hadi's stomach fell out from beneath him. "Hadi…"

"You make it a point to sleep with all your suspects?" Hadi threw out, frowning at the floor. He felt the heat building up in his neck, ears burning and fought it down, until he felt the pain in his right palm.

"Hadi, that's not how it is," James said, coming back out of the kitchen towards Hadi. Hadi stepped back. "Please, I know how this looks."

"I doubt it," Hadi said, turning on his heel. He didn't want to be anywhere near James Kendall. He felt the doorknob give beneath his grip and heard the door slam as he fled back down the stairs.

~

"...mommy said no, Joshua. Put Nana back on the phone. - - Right now!" Valerie barked into her phone. She sighed heavily, rubbing the bridge of her nose. Now was not the time for her children to have the epic meltdown of all meltdowns. She had a job to do and needed the focus to be on that job not on her tyrannical three-year-old. "Joshua James!"

She bumped into someone as she spoke, spinning around to offer an apology. What she saw made her do a double take. The young man she bumped was familiar to her, handsome with dark olive skin and hazel eyes; the second fire manipulator that James was supposed to be tracking. That had ended in a complete fiasco, though James still tailed him. He was actually eerily good at his job. In fact, she was set to meet James later that evening to go over what they knew for certain. Five other fires had claimed too many lives since the train wreck. James suggested the arsonist would be a first responder, someone *always* at the scene but, so far, that gave them fifteen different names and none of them pinged on the Evolved registry. Not that anyone expected them to. The registry was painfully limited because people did not openly admit to being Evolved. It was generally considered bad for one's health to admit such things. Being openly gay was more widely accepted than being Evolved.

"Mom, I'll call you back. Don't give him any ice cream," Valerie said in a rush, ending the call as she stuffed the phone into her back pocket. She had no front pockets and the ones in her short coat were not adequate enough to hold the large smart phone without having it drop to the pavement every time she took a step. It was incredibly frustrating; incredibly distracting. "Excuse me!"

"Yeah?" the young man said, turning to look at her. He did not look like a killer or carry himself like some arrogant ass. He carried himself like a twenty-something kid trying to make a living. She looked him over, flushing when he arched an eyebrow at her.

"Sorry... thought you were someone else," she said, letting his elbow go. He shrugged it off and walked up the steps to the library carrying several books beneath his arm. She did not like doubting James, but he was too close, losing focus. Virgil had completely ruined any hope of secrecy for James, something Valerie felt partially responsible for. Her best friend had been sulking since their 'break up'; not that they were ever a 'thing'. Still, she saw where the attraction was. As soon as the thought left her mind, the library exploded with such force she went flying across the street.

The ringing in her ears was deafening. That high-pitched echo was the only thing that reached her mind by way of sound. She felt pain at her back, a tenderness that made her wince and move slowly. She could smell acrid smoke, feel the heat of flames behind her. Somewhere in her periphery, she was aware of people running. Something told her to look up, to look for the man named Hadi.

She found him, kneeling on the floor a few feet from her with books toppled all around him. People around them suddenly caught fire as they ran, thrashing around on the ground as if that might spare them. The bartender looked as startled as Valerie was, reaching out towards them to pull the flames *away*. He was helping them.

Valerie turned to look behind her and felt her blood run cold. Another man stood at the top of the steps, hands stuffed into pockets. He wore a dark mask but was tall and broad in the shoulder. Two other explosions ripped across the library's courtyard, sending waves of sharp, burning glass out into the crowd.

"Looks like I caught me a little Sparrow," the masked figure said. She did not hear his voice, not really. She felt the vibrations of it, peered at the dark eyes behind the mask. She knew this man, knew his face and eyes but her mind was so fogged with pain she could not force any coherent thought to the surface. Another pyro, maybe? She looked for the young bartender again, unable to lay eyes on him this time.

Her head hurt and her back throbbed. They'd been tipped off that three locations in Chicago received threats: Chicago Library, Mercy Hospital and Medical Center, and Shedd Aquarium. Various teams had been dispatched to each location but Valerie had been closest to the library so she arrived before the rest of the team. If she was right in her guestimation, they were still at least fifteen minutes out.

"Don't," Valerie warned, pulling her gun from her back holster. She aimed it at the perpetrator's head as best she could despite the ringing in her ears that was creating undulating vertigo all around her. The man in the mask merely laughed at her. He said something else but she could not make it out. In fact, her attention was focused behind him, on the burning building, on the people engulfed in flames. She felt hot just watching it, sweat running down her face and down the valley of her breasts. Suddenly she realized what was coming and gritted her teeth against the rising heat that would eventually end in her demise.

"STOP IT!!" someone else hollered. It was loud enough and brash enough for Valerie to hear it through the ringing in her ears. She could hear other things too, she noticed: screaming and the distinct pop-crackle of fire or the thunderous booms of new explosions.

"Leave her alone!" the same someone said.

The masked man looked both annoyed and amused at whoever spoke. Valerie could not find the will to turn around. She still burned inside, still wanted to fall to the ground and die. She had to fight it. She thought of her children: Joshua, who was only three; Anne-Marie who was five; Adam who wasn't even one yet. They'd already lost their father; she needed to fight for them.

"The little fire bird. Fucking everything up," the masked man said. Valerie heard it as a muffled mess, but a muffled mess that she recognized. She knew the voice. "Time to die, little fire bird."

Valerie couldn't hold on anymore. She was vaguely aware of being hauled to her feet though she did not have the energy to remain standing. She barely had the energy to keep her eyes open. She wracked her memory for the voice she recognized, the dark eyes and - brows. Angelo. That was the last thing she remembered, hearing the explosions continue in the background as everything went black.

09

James ran through the hospital hallways, heedless of who might shout at him or the dirty looks he received from those he shoved aside. He ran straight to the ICU where several other A.E.C. agents hovered, all of them speaking to different doctors, nurses or eyewitnesses that only sustained minor injuries. They were not done collecting charred corpses out of the downtown library, the medical center or the aquarium. All three targets had been hit simultaneously - a detraction from the normal arson fires of late. The death toll would be astronomical.

This was no longer a single arsonist hired by some sick Evolved piece of shit. This was now a coordinated effort with inside information that *only* A.E.C. agents were privy to. Things were getting worse. This time, witnesses identified one of the perpetrators - a young man with hazel eyes that controlled some of the fires.

"Where is she?" James interjected drawing the circle of attention to himself.

"Agent Falcon, now is not the time," one of the suits said. James snarled and grabbed him by his perfectly pressed lapel.

"Where. Is. She, *Duck*?" he repeated through gritted teeth.

"In surgery, Agent Falcon."

James stopped, letting Duck go. The idiot brushed his coat off as if he were contaminated with dust just by being touched. A short woman in her sixties approached the group with a stern look in her eyes followed by Zephyr in all her 'haughty spunk' and then some. The elder woman, Special Agent Gloria "Osprey" Marcus, ran the A.E.C. with a firm hand. She founded the PeaceKeepers and, rumor was, that she was one of the most powerful Evolved walking the earth. None of it mattered to James.

"I need your head clear, Falcon," Marcus said evenly. James opened his mouth to argue but Osprey forestalled him. "She's got severe burns that are taking their toll. She's too weak, weaker than she should be. The Collector was there, we're sure of it. There are more dead at the library than either of the other two locations, not all of them were burned. Autopsies should confirm our theories but that will take time."

"He wanted the focus at the library," Zephyr said. Her accent, he noted, sounded a little on the rough side, as if she'd not slept but still held hints of her high level of education and snobbery. It was mind-boggling. "Everyone saw your boy, Agent Falcon. Everyone. What we're now trying to determine is why."

James frowned and shook his head. "Hadi is *not* a killer. If he was there, it was coincidence."

"Isn't it your job to follow that freak?" Duck cut in, folding his arms across his chest.

"I was on route to the hospital, per *your* orders, ma'am," James said, directing his statement to Zephyr. She pursed her lips at him but did not argue. She *had* given him such an order. Valerie was already close to the library at the time, so she took point there; James took point at the hospital, and one of the PeaceKeepers, Ronin - the woman all in black - took the aquarium.

Something had gone wrong. Someone had to be feeding the Collector and whoever he had under his thumb information from the inside. It had to be. That was the only explanation. James refused to believe that Hadi would be involved with any of it, no matter what was at stake or offered.

"The good little soldier, always following orders," Duck teased. James grit his teeth so hard his jaw clicked.

"My *partner* is fighting for her life, Angelo," James snarled. Valerie had just lost her husband to cancer less than a year prior. She had three babies that needed her; three babies that were going to ask why their mommy wasn't coming home that night. It broke his heart just thinking about them.

"The doctors will do what they can," Zephyr said. "We've got a few tricks up our sleeves. Neurophage is in there with them. Right now, I need you to focus. Something went wrong. I think you're on to something with your first responder theory."

"Agent Zephyr-" James began.

"Just call me Z. Agent never set well with me," she said. He arched a brow but continued on.

"Fine, with no offense intended, what does my theory have to do with Sparrow or whatever the fuck just happened out there. In case you didn't notice, *three* differ- ent buildings just blew up! At the same time! My theory be dammed! There is *no way* two Evolved could have pulled that off on their own."

"Are you suggesting you think your man had something to do with this?" Zephyr said, cocking her hip to the side.

"No! I don't know! Look, what I think very clearly doesn't matter to anyone and right now he's being hunted like some rabid dog! Whoever this is is still killing peo- ple, still out there wreaking havoc, and *no one* is doing anything about it. She shouldn't have been alone, not with the tip-off we got. She's got kids waiting for her at home, dammit! Instead of looking for the *correct* perp, you've all been more concerned about harassing a bartender!"

Duck tossed a glare at James for the comment about the bartender. It had been Duck's assessment that dragged James out of Arizona to monitor Hadi in the first place. While he certainly enjoyed the young man's com- pany, it was clear from the very beginning that he was not a threat and their resources in following him were being wasted. Even now, with the things the witnesses had seen, James had to believe that Hadi simply ended up in the wrong place at the wrong time.

"The same could be said for you, Falcon," Duck threw in, plucking invisible lint from his crisp overcoat. "That bartender has had an awful lot of your attention lately. I hope he's put out for you."

James threw the first punch, connecting solidly with Angelo's jaw. Unfairly, the other two that always hovered around Duck retaliated on their leader's behalf, taking James back several steps so that he could not lunge forward and give Duck another fist to the face.

"Gentlemen!" Zephyr barked, placing herself between the two brawlers. "This is neither the time nor the place for petty squabbles. Pull your heads out of your asses and focus! Angelo, take a walk!"

"Are you blind! He hit me first!" Angelo argued.

"NOW!" Zephyr hollered, earning the ire of the nursing staff on hand. Agent Osprey backed her by arching a brow at Angelo and his crones, chasing them out with a single look.

"There is a traitor among us, Agent Falcon," Zephyr continued after Angelo had gone. "As awful as it is to say, we're lucky that the only one seriously injured was Agent Sparrow. This could have been much worse."

That was not what James wanted to hear. They had flubbed this entire operation up, looking in the wrong direction from day one. First Hadi, now Valerie. James clenched his jaw, nostrils flaring in agitation. He wanted to see Valerie, wanted to find answers.

"Are you with us, or not, Agent Falcon?" Zephyr continued. "I need someone that I can trust."

"I'm with you," James growled under his breath.

"Good. Find Hadi Shahir."

James frowned at her.

"Do you trust him?" Zephyr pressed. James was not sure how to answer that, but nodded all the same. "He saw what Agent Sparrow did. *I* trust *you.* Find your bartender and we'll have our answers."

~

A somber gloom settled over the 13th Hour. Mondays were notoriously slow, but, for some reason, this particular Monday felt *dead*. Lindy wiped down the bar and the tables, even cleaned the vinyl seats of the chairs and booths. Greg sat in his normal seat, but he was the only one in the bar that night.

"Haze," Greg slurred, already on his second bottle of bourbon. "Refill."

"Haze, ain't here, Greg," Lindy said sadly. Hadi left a message for her earlier that morning, apologizing for any trouble he'd brought to her or Tam, to the bar. He put in his notice, effective immediately, and asked that she look after Amir. She'd finally turned the TV off when the only thing running were the tragedies throughout the city. Four days and that was all anyone talked about; that and the man that caught fire outside the library. Lindy sighed, thinking about Hadi, hoping he was safe. She refilled Greg's glass, looking up hopefully when the bell above the door rang. Her hope shattered, replaced with livid anger when she saw who walked through the door.

"He's not here, *Agent* Kendall," Lindy snipped.

Greg went so far as to twist around to look over his shoulder as if seeing someone new.

"Where is he, Lindy?" James demanded. Lindy shook her head at him, waggling a finger as she moved out from behind the bar to square off with the man they'd accepted as family; the man who lied to them.

"Nuh-uh, no, you don't get to treat me like a criminal. I said he ain't here and I don't know where he is. Wouldn't tell you if I did. So you can take your fancy title and your fancy dog and get out of my bar."

James looked down at Gen who did not understand the complexities of human relationships. She glanced up at Lindy, her big brown puppy dog eyes begging for a treat or a pat on the head. James did not have time for sassy attitude. Lindy did not care.

"Lindy, I'm trying to help him."

"You've got a real shitty way of showin' it," Lindy threw back. She waited for an argument, arms folded but he did not give her one. "Just leave, *Agent*. Ain't nobody 'round here what needs your kind of help."

"This is a public place," he argued feebly. She glared at him and pointed her middle finger at the sign above the door. It read 'We reserve the right to refuse service to anyone.'

James sighed and left the bar. He stopped outside, popping a bottle of extra strength Tylenol so he could toss back four of the tiny white pills at once. Every part of him hurt for more reasons than one. He'd been splitting his time and attention between work and Valerie's kids. Explaining *that* to them was one of the most difficult things he'd ever done. He was not sleeping well and still needed to find Hadi. Then, suddenly, it struck him. He glanced up

to the windows above the bar, moving around to the door
at the rear of the building where the entrance to the apartments was. He took the steps two at a time, Genevieve
following after him with a jingling collar, before stopping
in front of a closed door.

"Amir!" James called, pounding on the door to
Hadi's apartment. "Amir! I know you're there, kid. Ami-"

The door opened, cutting James off mid-holler.

Amir stood in the door, looking less than im-
pressed. James couldn't blame him. The smell of incense
and ramen wafted out into the hallway. Despite knowing
Hadi for several months now, he'd never been to the kid's
apartment. It was small, cozy, and in desperate need of a
maid.

"He's not here, Agent Kendall."

James silently cursed the day he accepted recruit-
ment from the A.E.C.

"Please tell me you know something about where
he might be, Amir."

Amir shook his head, turning to go back into
the apartment. He left the door open, so James followed.
Music played in the background, too soft for James to
tell what kind, only that the melody was soothing. There
were pictures on the wall and three mismatched barstools
against the kitchen. The layout was not all that dissimilar
to James' place, if a little more cramped and dingy. The
incense masked the heavy smell of pot, and the counter
had a tiny dish of questionable white powder that James
was positive was not used for washing dishes.

"I dunno," Amir sighed. "Give it time, you have

everyone in Chicago hunting him down."

"It's standard operating procedure after something like that happens. I didn't put the order in. Please, Amir."

"You still think he blew up the library?" Amir questioned. James opened his mouth but then sighed and shook his head. He flapped his arms helplessly. He didn't know what to think. The evidence was damming but James had severe doubts; it just wasn't in Hadi's nature. "Let me show you something."

James followed Amir back to a bedroom piled floor to ceiling with books and magazines, charts, or miniature pieces of artworks. There was a small record player on the dresser and a stack of vinyls on the floor beside it, along with more questionable paraphernalia that James chose to ignore. Everyone had their demons. "Is this your throne room?"

"It's not mine," Amir said gently. He spoke in softer tones than Hadi, his accent a little thicker but no less alluring. "It's Hadi's. Any book, any page, ask him to tell you what's on it and he will tell you word for word. Any record, he can sing for you or play on that stupid keyboard he keeps under his bed after hearing it only once. He is the smartest man that I know. Do you really think he would do something so awful as blow up knowledge?"

James felt like an ass. He hadn't known this part of Hadi. There was nothing in the files about a young man with eidetic memory, or a thirst for knowledge. It was not random knowledge either. There were books on religion and philosophy, science, and history. He had full fantasy series, or historical fiction, even a few romance novels.

The music was just as varied, from Mozart to the Beatles, and Marilyn Manson.

"I need to talk to him, Amir. It is *so* important. The only other person I trust is fighting for her life right now. Hadi saw what she did. I need to know what he saw; *who* he saw; what happened at that library. No one will give us a clear answer. And… I need you to talk to Lindy."

"Lindy? Why?" Amir asked, walking back out to the living room. James followed feeling oddly like an intruder.

"I need to talk to her boyfriend."

"You think her boyfriend did this?" Amir asked incredulously. James shook his head, rubbing his face in exasperation.

"No, no… Hadi said something about it the night he stayed at my place. He said she was dating a fireman. It's been nagging at me ever since. I think… I think the guy setting all these fires is a first responder; a firefighter. Which means, Lindy's boyfriend has probably talked to this guy; probably a lot. He might know something, have seen something that could indicate an Evolved. But, she won't give me the time of day."

Amir looked at him. His phone chimed twice, indicating a text. He looked at James, then at the phone. James shrugged, letting him answer the text.

"It's Lindy," Amir said. "Hadi's coming to the bar tonight."

"Amir…"

"I'll talk to her."

10

The 13th Hour was James Kendall's second home. He knew it as well as his own one-bedroom apartment, even made suggestions for new scents to be placed in the bathrooms that were not as caustic as 'evergreen dream' or 'cinnamon swirl'. However, standing in the dark hall that led back to those same bathrooms suddenly made him feel like an intruder. Zephyr - now known to him more casually as Z - stood beside him, idly tapping her fingers together.

The rest of her team positioned themselves at various points around the 13th Hour or in locations nearby should Hadi try to run. Somewhere inside, James felt that the whole situation was wrong; Hadi was not a criminal, he felt that in his marrow.

"Penny for your thoughts, Agent Falcon," Zephyr said, interrupting James' brooding mind.

"You don't have enough pennies," he shot back.

His voice was pitched low, a croaking whisper while they hid, waiting and hoping Amir did not lead them astray.

"This isn't your cup of tea, is it?" she persisted. He gave her a sidelong glance but kept silent. He was not really in the mood for idle conversation. She was the type of woman who persisted until you wanted to scream, however, so he answered.

"I'm a soldier, Zephyr," he said, not comfortable with her insistence on being so casual. "I follow orders and don't normally question. What I did - I regret. It wasn't right. We're chasing down an innocent man like he's vermin - to what end? Our job is to protect the populace, to make sure the Evolved *don't* get out of hand, not to cage them up like animals in a zoo. This entire thing has just... I doubt you'd appreciate the situation as much if roles were reversed."

She remained blessedly silent for a time then nodded. "No, I suppose I wouldn't."

James glanced at her but remained silent. He'd said his piece. His attention was diverted by the sound of mumbled voices. He heard Lindy clear as day, but the others were softer, deeper. James dared a peek around the corner. Amir blocked some of his view, but Virgil Krisken stood like a monolith above the smaller group. Lindy was there and, presumably, Hadi as well, but James couldn't see him. It was Virgil that threw him off. James did not expect to see the large ex-con there. Amir was apologizing to Hadi in Arabic; James could hear his soft, shame-filled words.

"For what?" Hadi asked, giving James his cue to stop skulking like a rat in a dark alley.

"For me, Hadi," James said as he stepped out around the corner. "He's sorry for me."

"You little ass!" Lindy screeched, slapping Amir on the back of the head. "You called them!"

"We're outta here," Virgil said, placing a large, beefy hand on Hadi's shoulder so that he could be tucked in front of Virgil's very imposing form.

"Sit down, Crush," Zephyr said, joining James in the main bar area. "Yes, I'm well aware of who you are. We're only here to talk."

"Girlfriend?" Hadi snapped, directing his ire at Zephyr though the question was meant for James.

"Hardly," she replied evenly. "You can call me Z."

Hadi's eyebrow shot up, arms folded across his chest. Amir hovered nearby, as protective of Hadi as Virgil and Lindy, but less volatile than the other two. *He,* at least, maintained a calm exterior no matter what the situation presented.

"I need to know what happened at the library, Hadi," James said gently. Hadi frowned, practically sneering at James. "Please. I need to know what you saw; *who* you saw."

"Ask the asshole with the eyebrows," Hadi barked. "You know, the *other* pyro-Evolved that tried to torch that lady I took to the hospital."

James frowned. This was not in the report. Victims of the blast were all carried in by first-responders or treated in emergency triage tents. And the only Evolved reported on sight was Hadi.

"Who filed the report?" James said, looking at Zephyr in her business casual attire with a sword strapped to her back. His job was nothing if not interesting.

"Angelo," she said through a heavy breath. And, suddenly, everything clicked into place. James could see it in her bright green eyes, the way she turned her head slowly to meet his gaze, knowing he came to the same conclusion. Angelo Gustavo was their mole *and* an Evolved.

"MJ," Virgil said quietly with fingers pressed to his ear. The lights inside the bar cut out. Everything was plunged into pitch black darkness. James heard Lindy complain, was aware of movement, but could not see anything beyond the tip of his own nose.

"Shit. Hadi!" he called into the darkness. No one responded; not that he expected them to. Instead, he grabbed Zephyr's wrist - or, what he hoped was her wrist - and tugged towards where he remembered the front door to be. It took a few stumbling steps and a couple of squashed toes, but he finally found the handle, breathing a sigh of relief when he heard the familiar jingling of the bell above his head. Both he and Zephyr burst out of the bar in time to see a suped-up Dodge speed away down the main street, nearly taking two other cars out in the process.

"Dammit!" Zephyr cursed, whirling where she stood so that James had no choice but to follow or have his arm ripped out of socket. "Ronin, I need a tail on a Dodge Charger, neon racing stripes, covered plates heading south on South Green Bay Avenue towards east 108th Street. Karma, link us up - pull Falcon in as well."

"Pull me into-" James could not finish his sentence. His mind was suddenly spinning with thoughts of at least seven other people, probably more if he really took the time to listen.

"You could have waited until *after* I gave him a transmitter patch, Karma," Zephyr said. He felt pressure just behind his ear, a wild wave of vertigo that made him wretch and then blessed silence.

"My apologies, Agent Falcon. I assumed Zephyr had already tapped you in," a familiar male voice said.

Zephyr made a face of annoyance but ran around to a side alley two buildings over and mounted a rather impressive motorcycle.

"On," she ordered. James was not in any mood to argue, frowning at the woman's new outfit. Somewhere in his delirium, she had changed from business casual to a stylized form of Valkyrie armor. "Hang on!"

James did as commanded, squeezing tight to Zepyhr's middle while simultaneously trying to avoid the *pixie wings and sword* at her back. Yes, his job was *very* interesting.

"Black Myst - Eric, are you online?" Zephyr said. James heard her voice, though he was also aware that the wind howled in his ears as they gave chase, cars honking at them or pedestrians hollering for them to slow down.

"Read ya' loud n' clear beautiful, whatcha need?" came another disembodied voice.

"Track down Angelo Gustavo. Retain at all cost; headless counts. Hunt with caution, the idiot is Evolved. Pyro."

"Roger that, boss-lady. Myst out."

~

Hadi stared out the back window of the Charger, noting how dark it was. There were no lights anywhere, creating a cluster of cars and pedestrians, people peeking out from windows with flashlights or store owners hovering in their doorways. Amir and Lindy sat with him, Virgil in the front seat with a girl Hadi had been introduced to only the day before in the driver's seat. The car was specially designed for her specific needs, one of the most technologically advanced vehicles he'd ever seen. Part of him expected it to talk. If he weren't running for his life, he might have asked if it did.

"Hadi," Amir began sadly, head hanging to his chest.

"It's ok," he said before Amir could finish.

He rubbed his brother's shoulders and offered an understanding grin. Amir was only trying to help.

"Y'all, how in all of flying shit storms is any of this ok?" Lindy asked. Hadi looked at her but had no answer. The entire situation was beyond ludicrous, but that was not the easiest thing to admit *or* put into words.

"V," Amir said, changing direction away from Hadi. "Why did that lady call you Crush?"

"Long story," Virgil answered. It was a story for another time. Racing through the darkened streets of East Side Chicago was not the time for stories to be told.

"We're being followed," MJ said. Hadi liked her. She was young, but smart as a whip and didn't let anything stop her. The car was all hers, modified for her needs, painted, upgraded. He'd seen some of her other techy toys too and marveled at all of them. "Two teams; PeaceKeepers and someone else."

No one said anything, looking around the car at each other as MJ dodged a trash truck that ran through the blinking intersection light. Their silent looks tried to make sense out of things, devise a plan without actually speaking or, maybe, just wrap their minds around what was currently happening. They were fugitives; all of them. Somehow, Hadi had roped Amir and Lindy into the chaos that had become of his life. He looked at them both, saw the concern and fear on their faces, then looked at Virgil.

"MJ," he said. "Swing back around and head north. Go to the Bean."

"What? Why?" she asked, daring to glance over her shoulder. That's all it took. A split second and all of them were screaming, screeching metal ringing in their ears or shards of glass tearing through their flesh. They rolled and flipped, the roof of the car, squashing down until Hadi felt it pressing on his skull. He braced himself on the back of the driver's seat and the one bar that remained intact, watching the sparks fly as they skid across the road. Eventually, they came to a stop, the car teetering on its top like an overturned turtle.

There was a crackle of voices that echoed out into the night, squealing tires and honking horns from other vehicles that tried to avoid the totaled Charger. They were hit twice, spinning in circles or skidding across the pavement to bank against a flickering lamp post. Hadi could smell gas, and his ears were ringing, shoulders sore from where the seatbelt dug in.

"Amir?" Hadi choked out, unable to twist around enough to see his little brother. "Lindy?"

"Present," Lindy said weakly. Relief rushed through half of Hadi, the other half tense and afraid for his brother. Hadi tried to move, tried to pry himself out of the seatbelt that held him upside down but failed. He heard slow, calculating footsteps and stopped moving, watching a pair of heavy black boots move toward the vehicle. He did his best to stay quiet, feeling a burn in his scarred palm that he pressed to the thick nylon of the seatbelt. He could smell it, feel it smolder beneath his hand, melting away thread by thread until it finally snapped. Hadi landed face first onto the crumpled roof of the car, scrambling backwards to relieve Amir and Lindy of their harnesses.

"I see you, little hellfire," a deep voice said. Hadi looked at Amir, unconscious and bleeding from his temples, then at Lindy, her face pale and eyes wide. "You've been a good scape goat but it's time for your story to come to a close."

Hadi looked at Lindy, shaking his head, pressing a finger to his lips. Tears flowed out of her eyes, but she remained quiet, grunting when Hadi finally burned through her straps. He put a hand over her mouth, scooting back with her beneath him until they were both out of the car on the opposite side. Virgil, Hadi noticed, was conscious but stuck. He jerked his head, silently ordering Hadi and Lindy to run, but Hadi shook his head. Much to his horror, Lindy stood up first.

"Lonny?" she sobbed. "You did this? You set all

those fires?"

Hadi ignored the conversation. It was enough of a distraction for him to get back into the car to free Amir and drag him out. Virgil had no straps holding him down, for he was too large to fit them. The vehicle cinched in around him, pinning him to the wreckage. Short of blowing the door off - and potentially hurting Virgil - Hadi could do nothing to help him.

"...Rae, please!" the booted man pleaded. Hadi peeked at him from time to time, or over at Lindy. He had his hands on the door frame, the warmth emanating from his palms working to soften the fiberglass and metal frame of the crushed up car. It was working. Virgil wiggled his shoulder enough to push the door out while Lindy vehemently shook her head and shouted at the man she called Lonny.

"A little more," Hadi whispered to Virgil, melting away more of the door frame until the man could shove the rest of it aside like it was a hunk of PlayDoh. Lindy squealed, hollering when Hadi grabbed her by the waist to pull her back down, switching spots with her. He threw a blast of flames at the elder man, catching him off guard long enough to scoop Amir up and dart away into an alley with Lindy following behind. He heard the crunch and tear of the car, followed by a grunted order to run. Hadi did not have to be told twice, throwing Amir over one shoulder so he could clamp on to Lindy's wrist and drag her along.

"Go!" Virgil hollered right as the alley lit up like a torch. Flames flew above and behind, coating the walls in fresh ash, and making the trash bins groan from the heat.

"Leave them alone!"

James. Hadi's steps slowed, watching the elder man literally *walk through* the flames that filled the alley. He fired a weapon at the other pyro-Evolved, the gunshot echoing against the brick walls.

"Lonny!"

"Going somewhere?" another voice cooed. The figure literally appeared out of nowhere, blocking the alley exit.

"Warlock!" Hadi heard. It was a woman that spoke, her very proper accent thick, even as it dripped with threats and anger. "What fuck up let you out of the Hole?"

"Hot pants!" the man dubbed Warlock said with a crooked smile. "Fancy meeting you here, cutie."

"Shut up, you wanker," she spat. "I'll only extend professional courtesy once: walk away."

"No can do, gorgeous. I got a job to do, just like you do."

Chaos exploded around Hadi. He felt someone grab the scruff of his shirt, dragging him sideways as Zephyr and Warlock went toe to toe. Heat brushed against Hadi's face, the fire blasting its way down the alley. Before Hadi knew what was happening, he was huddled in a corner with Amir slouched beside him, Lindy sobbing on his shoulder and MJ in his lap. Virgil and James made quick work of the pyro-Evolved, shoving him into a trash bin that Virgil literally smashed shut. Warlock and Zephyr fought, grunting and screaming at each other while other figures darted around. Hadi heard sirens or alarms, shaking his head with hands over his ears. Everything over-

HELLFIRE

whelmed him, turning the entire alley into a pit of raging
fire.

11

"**Z**ephyr, report!" Karma shouted. He shared the same accent that she did, the same colloquialisms.

While he'd been doing this for much longer, he passed the torch of leadership to her when the vote came around. He was too old, too jaded to make the tactical decisions needed for the type of work the PeaceKeepers did. Case in point: she'd dropped communication over ten minutes prior and his blood pressure was now sky-rocketing. "Ronin?"

"I cannot reach her. There is too much fire. Warlock is here," the *youkai* woman said.

"Who is making the fire?" Karma demanded as he circled the state-of-the-art glass touch-panel desk to look over a young woman's shoulder. "WiFire I need visual."

The flat, transparent screens above the young woman popped to life with six different images, all different angles of the same location. The narrow alley between a bakery and a bank glowed bright orange. There were remnants of a crushed up vehicle leaning against the bakery wall and Zephyr's bike not far off.

"Dammit, girl…" Karma cursed, eyes darting between images on the screen. "Eric, Aerial - redirect to the following coordinates…"

"HADI!" James hollered, shaking the young man roughly by the shoulders. Lindy held on to the young girl MJ who, James learned, could not walk. Amir still slouched against the wall, sweat and blood mixing together at the temples. Every now and then James looked behind him where Zephyr still fought with some over-powered pop-rock, and he'd lost sight of Virgil entirely. Then he remembered the thing Zephyr had pushed into the back of his ear.

"Hey! Anyone there?" he hollered, though he was fairly certain the hollering was entirely unnecessary. "WHOA SHIT!"

A twisted metal ladder clattered just above his head, slamming into the ground beside Hadi. Ironically enough, that rocked the kid from his stupor, making him look up at James with fear and confusion on his young face.

"Get it together, man!" James hollered at him while reloading his gun. The fire immediately shrank to something a little less violent, making it easier for James to see. The fire didn't hurt him, but it sure as hell blinded the crap out of him. Staring into the sun did that, and his

eyesight wasn't what it used to be. He glanced around
the alley, noting the dueling pair at the far end, and took
aim. It took a little too long to calibrate his shot, but when
he pulled the trigger, it hit its mark. The idiot known as
Warlock took a good tumble to the left, giving Zephyr a
reprieve and pushing him out of the burning alley. That's
when James found Virgil again. The large man shoved a
metal trash bin over Warlock's head, backing up suddenly
when the ground exploded in a wild spray of blackened
tentacles.

"What the f—"

"Zephyr!" that familiar pretentious voice said in
James' head.

"She's hurt," James reported, marine training
making him press his fingers to the back of his ear as if to
activate whatever that little thingy was. Logically, he knew
that was unnecessary, but habit made him do it anyway.

"To whom am I speaking?" the voice demanded.

"Falcon," he answered, jogging over to Zephyr
to pull her back into the alley. She bled from the side, a
hole ripped through the armor with a piece of iron stair rail
shoved through her side. "This is gonna hurt."

That was the only warning he gave her, yanking
the rail out in one swift motion. She screamed, then glared
at him.

"Where's Haze?" Virgil asked, looming over
James and Zephyr like a giant ogre. James jerked his head
back to where he'd left them.

"In the burning vortex of hell," he said. "Hey,
disembodied voice - I need ideas here. We're a little, uhm,

overwhelmed and grossly underpowered. I've got an injured kid, a panicked waitress, a paraplegic techno-geek, a human bowling ball, and your little winged Valkyrie plus whatever just exploded out the ground to suck down that Warlock asshole. Aaaaand… I've got half a clip left. Options would be nice."

"Jimbo!" Virgil called, jerking his head toward another alley that was *not* on fire. He carried the girl that could not walk in one arm and had Amir slung over his other shoulder. Hadi stood beside him with Lindy clinging to him like glue, big streaks of black mascara running down her pale cheeks. James did not wait for a second option, scooping Zephyr up into his arms to follow Virgil. He stumbled, his leg choosing the worst moment ever to stiffen up and go unresponsive. Cursing under his breath, he forced compliance, hobbling after Virgil with an extra load in his arms.

"I'm fine," Zephyr insisted weakly.

"The hell you are," James bit back. "Just don't wiggle too much or I might drop you. Virgil! Where are we going?"

"Not here," the giant man answered. It was good enough for James. They hurried down the street, trying to be a little less noticeable than they were. Blessedly, they had the late hour on their side and a giant conflagration behind them that was drawing a great deal of attention *away* from them.

"Tsch!" someone hissed from a darker alley, barking at them in Japanese.

It took a moment for the word to translate in

James' mind. Hurry. Hurry where? His eyes darted around suspiciously, but saw nothing except Virgil moving on ahead.

"Virgil!" he hissed, making the large man stop. Hadi and Lindy turned around as well. "This better be one of your folks, Ms. Z."

"She is," Zephyr said with barely enough strength to make a whisper. He glanced down at her and sighed. He did not have time to build trust with talking shadows. He went into the alley, making sure Virgil, Hadi, and Lindy followed along. All he saw were the outlines of large trash bins until a single pair of pale gray eyes popped up right in front of him. He jumped in spite of himself but managed not to back away. Whoever it was put two slim fingers to Zephyr's pulse and looked at him.

"Come," she said. The woman in all black; Ronin. Now he knew her. He followed without question this time, walking deeper into the darkness. The pain he felt next made him cry out, falling back out of the dark with Zephyr still in his arms.

"James!"

James landed hard on the pavement. Zephyr rolled out of his arms, groaning. She did not move much, trying to push up to her knees but failing. Something hot and sharp had James by the shoulder, burning him from the inside out. That was something he could not shake off like he did other burning things. Minor powers were great when they were useful; this was not so useful.

"Lonny, stop it!" Lindy screeched. James could see her and Hadi, see Virgil and the girl that couldn't walk.

"I'm sorry, Lindsay-Rae."

Agony tore through James, making him scream.

He tried to pry the heat off of him, only to feel the burning hot metal sticking several inches out of his shoulder.

"JAMES!"

The dark street suddenly lit up like a firecracker. It hurt to keep his eyes open. It hurt anyway. James was aware of things groaning, of feeling steam rise up from the cracks in the pavement and panicked voices in his ear or head.

"…ent Falcon!!"

"Aerial, get over there!" someone else said.

"On it, broheim…"

James heard nothing else, finally passing out from the pain as the fire grew worse.

~

James jerked awake with a loud snort. His breath caught, making him choke. He coughed violently, rolling sideways to see a pristine white room with what he could only imagine were medical supplies and tissue boxes. Even the bed was white.

"Welcome back, Agent Falcon." Zephyr.

"Where am I?" James croaked. He continued to cough until Zephyr offered a drink of cool water that he guzzled. His shoulder was on fire and immobile, his head pounding and chest tight.

"PeaceKeeper headquarters," Zephyr answered. She let him drink more water, helping him to a seated position. "Thank you, by the way, for what you did."

James glanced at her, at the red spot on her shoulder and the bandage beneath the white tank she wore. She wore no mask, he realized, her brown hair in a simple braid that fell down her back. She was so young; like Hadi.

"Hadi-" James said suddenly, looking to her with panic twisting his stomach.

"We're looking," Zephyr explained. "Admittedly, the details are a little lost on me. From what I've been told, he lost his shit, burned five city blocks, and fled. We've been waiting for you, hoping you might have better luck reaching out to him than a full A.E.C. manhunt."

James remained quiet, taking things in. His arm was in a sling and he could feel the stitch and pull of bandages elsewhere on his person. The antiseptic smell he expected from a hospital or even a medical center was oddly absent, as were any tubes or wires that might detect heart rate or deliver oxygen. His right arm flexed absently, the muscles twitching terribly and then relaxing after a gentle breeze from above. Interesting.

"How long have I been here?" he asked.

"Three days," Zephyr sighed. "How many languages do you speak, Falcon?"

He looked up at her, frowning. "What difference does it make?"

"Humor me," she persisted, folding her arms beneath her breasts.

"Eight."

She considered his answer, nodding silently, but said nothing more. Instead, she handed James his phone before walking out. The silence that lingered made his frown deepen. She had not given an order, only planted a thought. She was good. James glanced at his phone. On the back was a sticky note that said 'Neuro likes your dog. She misses you. Karma won't let her inside headquarters. Sorry.'

James sighed, leaning back on his pillows. It hurt to move, hurt to breathe, hurt to think. He remembered the transmitter Zephyr slapped on him and touched the back of both ears. There was nothing there. He looked at the phone again and turned it on. It was singed on one corner and the screen was cracked, but it still worked. He had four missed calls, but no new texts. His thumb went to the circle with Hadi's face on his contacts, hovering briefly before pulling up the text window.

ARE YOU SAFE?

It took thirty minutes for a response to come through.

R U OK??

James grinned. A surprising amount of relief turned his muscles to jelly, robbing him of all energy. He slept for a good hour before forcing himself out of bed. It didn't take long to find clothes or an exit, though it took some creativity to find his way back to the city - and a borrowed motorcycle that Zephyr could fire him for later.

To her credit, the bike was rather exceptional. It handled well, auto-adjusting to his weight rather than hers. Several displays told him things like speed and tire pressure, battery level - yeah, one of those fancy electric things - and fuel reserve. But they also read off his heart rate, weight, outside temperature, and wind velocity.

"Nice," he said into the helmet that had also au-to-adjusted to fit him.

"Glad you approve, Agent Falcon."

James nearly lost control of the bike. The panel that displayed his heart rate spiked, flashing bright red for a moment. Other vehicles sped by, honking at him for his erratic driving.

"If you crash my bike, you're paying for a new one."

"Do you get perverse joy out of invading a guy's privacy, Agent Z?" James sighed, focusing on the road.

"You stole my bike," Zephyr countered.

"Borrowed," James corrected. "What'd you do, slap me with another sticker thing when I wasn't looking?"

"The transmitter is in the helmet," he heard Zephyr giggle.

"Of course it is," he groaned. He sped past de-livery vehicles and the lake shore, knowing he was being monitored. He didn't care. He needed to bring some clo-sure to things, to undo the mess that he'd tangled himself in, to speak to Hadi man to man, not agent to Evolved.

"Care to share your destination, Agent Falcon?"

"I'm sure you'll figure it out," James snipped. He could almost feel the smile on her face. She had an unusu-al interest in him he had yet to puzzle out. A problem for another time. As soon as James reached the city limits, he revved the speed and headed straight for Millennium Park. The Bean reflected tourists and locals alike, gleaming in weak sunlight.

"What day is it, Agent Z?" James asked as he

parked.

"Saturday," she answered just before he removed the helmet. He rolled his right shoulder, flexing his hand. Maneuvering a bike with one arm took skill regardless of how tech happy the thing was. James ignored the pain, walking around slowly until finding his target.

Hadi sat alone on a stone bench, looking at the Bean. He wore fashionably torn jeans - if such a thing were possible - a button down, and sneakers so white they were blinding. It was entirely unlike Hadi.

"If you're trying to blend in, you're not doing a very good job," James said as he sat on the bench beside the young bartender. He sat calmly, keeping his distance so as not to spook Hadi into running or worse. There were too many people around for 'or worse'.

"How'd you find me?" Hadi frowned. James shot him a flat stare.

"Despite what you might think of me, I do genuinely pay attention to what you say and do. Your two favorite places are the library and the Bean. Process of elimination did the rest. You're taking a big risk being out here, Hadi."

"I could say the same for you," he countered. "New orders, or just visiting, Agent Kendall?" James winced. He deserved that. "How many of your new friends do you have around this time?"

James shrugged. "A few probably; one for sure. Please let us help you, Hadi."

"Help me?" he crowed, turning slightly to face James. Rage filled his eyes, burnishing them a soft orange instead of the beautiful hazel they normally were. "Since I've been here, all you people want to do is kill me or arrest me. Why? What in the Hell did I do to any of you? This entire country is fucked up and I can't even leave anymore! Not that you care…"

"Do you really think I'd be here if I didn't care?" James threw back. He kept his voice low, watching everyone, but his temper was rising. "Yes, we fucked up; *I* fucked up, ok? I'm sorry. We're human, Hadi. We make mistakes."

"Ruining my life is a pretty big mistake, James," Hadi said rising to his feet.

"Then let me help you f-fi - - fuck!" James cursed, feeling his arm twitch and words cleave to the roof of his mouth. He flexed his right hand again, shaking his entire arm out. He was aware of Hadi returning to the bench and looked down when he heard the distinct rattle of pills. Hadi said nothing, holding James's meds out for him.

"Lindy said we had to take care of Gen," Hadi explained softly. "They were just sitting on the counter. I don't know why I grabbed them. I doubt they have James meds at Superdouche Castle."

"Thanks," James mumbled, taking the bottle then frowning. "Zephyr said someone else was taking care of Gen."

"Well, they weren't doing a good job," Hadi snorted. "Lindy took her to my place."

"Your place? Hadi, why the Hell would you go there? People are *looking* for you you!"

"Cuz I don't wanna wear stolen clothes, ok?" Hadi

bit back. "Amir went with her, she's not alone."

James only sighed, swallowing two of his pills dry. He stuffed the bottle in his pocket and stood up. "Come on, I'll take you home so you can get your stuff. I can get you a ticket out to Oregon or somewhere west. There isn't a big A.E.C. presence in Oregon or Utah."

Hadi looked up at him, skeptical and wary. He had right to be. James was done lying or begging, though. He was done trying to walk the righteous path. There was no such thing. He walked towards the bike instead, hoping Hadi would follow. Eventually, the bartender trotted along behind him, hands in pockets, blinding shoes lighting him up like a neon globe.

"Don't you need to take me to Superdouche Castle?" Hadi asked. James shook his head.

"I wasn't given any orders, Hadi. I just want to help and, right now, that means getting you as far from here as I can."

"Won't you get fired?"

James rolled his eyes and rounded on the poor kid behind him. "Do you want my help or don't you? Yeah, I'll probably get fired. I'm too old for this shit, anyway. Not that it matters cuz you won't actually believe anything I say. I get it. I messed up. Know that I care enough to get you somewhere safe, at least, so you don't end up dead, or - or - ugh! Dammit! To Hell with it."

James grabbed Hadi by the shirt and kissed him; hard. He let it linger just long enough, then shoved away. "Get on the damn bike."

He caught the slightest of grins on Hadi's face as

he slipped the helmet on and mounted the bike, glad when Hadi climbed on behind him.

"Interesting tactic, Agent Falcon," he heard and glared.

"You shut up."

"What!" Hadi said.

"Not you!"

"Bring him in, Falcon," Zephyr said as James kicked off and sped away from Millenium Park.

"Yeah…" James sighed, pulling the helmet off and tossing it aside. "Bite me."

Hadi only laughed and squeezed a little harder around James's middle.

12

Angelo Gustavo polished the barrel of the silencer on his favorite weapon with the edge of his shirt. Blood already soaked the carpet in the small apartment above the 13th Hour, but that was neither here nor there for Angelo. He'd commandeered one of the tall barstools for his guest. The man sagged in his seat, head lolling to his chest. Blood ran from his temple and into the thick, salted beard growing on the man's face. Angelo checked on him, made sure he was still breathing and all. Lonny failed to do his job, for sure, but Angelo still kinda liked the guy. He was mostly decent people with a good eye for business and a decent lack of morality. Like so many others, however, he suffered from an excess of personal attachment.

"And that's where it got ya, Lonny-boy," Angelo said to the unconscious man. "Now we have to kill the dimwit waitress too. Shame, that. She looks like she might be a good piece of ass to have. That's why you kept her around, ain't it? Usually is. That was Kendall's downfall too. Sex is man's greatest bane, Lonny."

Angelo left the unconscious man be, double checking the few blinking devices that had been strategically placed around the apartment. Fourth floor, it wouldn't take much to bring the entire building down. A nice bit of mayhem. He peeked out the front window, making a crack in the blinds. Across the street, the little apartment complex looked dead to the world, smashed between a dry-cleaner and a deli, and shrouded in thick fog that rolled in off the lake after the morning's rain.

Rain was good. Rain worked to Angelo's advantage. He saw the shifting shadows in the alley too. Peace-Keepers. Assholes. They'd been around for the last hour. Well, he had a surprise for them too.

He walked back into the kitchen, pulling a beer from the refrigerator. Guinness. At least the kid had decent taste in beer. With a bit of time to kill, Angelo plopped himself down on the Ikea-esque couch, winced at how stiff it was, and channel surfed until finally settling on *Die Hard.* He kept the gun beside him, an extra clip in the leather holster he wore. This was the part of his job he liked the best: the anticipation right before the kill.

The phone at Angelo's hip vibrated, making him glance down at it. It was time. He thumbed the alarm off and pulled out a pair of leather gloves that he kept in his back pocket. He slipped each finger into the glove, stretching it, relishing the feel of how tight it felt on his hand.

"Show time, Lonny-boy" Angelo said as he stood

up. He walked over to where Lonny sagged in the barstool and snatched the iPhone off the counter in front of the other man.

"Really, Lon? iPhone? Pussy."

Very calmly, Angelo unlocked the phone, thumbing through the contacts while swaying to the score played during the action sequences of *Die Hard*. He mouthed some of the words, too, not hurried in the least. When he finally found the number he sought, he grinned and began reading some of the messages to get an idea of how the pyro-Evolved spoke. Once he had it down, he leaned against the counter to compose a text.

WE NEED TO LEAVE. IT ISN'T SAFE. PLEASE, BABY. I'M SORRY. I LOVE YOU. MEET ME AT THE BAR. - LONNY

"Such a sap, Lonny," Angelo said, shaking his head. He pocketed the phone, collecting some things that caught his attention and proceeded to walk towards the bedroom with all the books and cocaine; he pocketed that too, feeling its weight in his coat. He adjusted the lapels on his coat, smoothed back his jet- black hair and counted to twenty. All things considered, the waitress wasn't *that* dimwitted and probably a little more than upset at her soon-to-be ex-boyfriend.

At exactly twenty, Angelo stepped out through the bedroom door, raised the barrel of his gun, and fired. He ignored the little whines and sobs that preceded the high-pitched whir of the silenced bullet. It went straight through the girl's skull. His other guest howled behind a dirty rag stuffed in his mouth, tied as the waitress had been, and sobbed. Prick.

"Patience, pumpkin," Angelo said, leveling the barrel of his silencer at his other hostage's head. "Your turn will come soon."

Angelo untied the waitress and carried her limp body to the living room. Her eyes remained wide, confused, and frightened as he set her on the floor, a clean hole center mass right between the eyes. Angelo then untied Lonny, watching with sick satisfaction as the big idiot fell on top of his blond whore. He then went back to the bedroom and hauled the Arab kid to his feet. Were they Arabic? Not that it really mattered. Both were expendable just like the rest of their turban-headed relatives. Angelo dragged the kid to the back alley and stuffed him in the trunk, banging on it once to get him to shut up and stop kicking the inside of his car. He then, very calmly, walked back up to the apartment, lighting up one of the joints he'd pilfered from the room with all the books with just a snap of his fingers. So much good stuff in there. Part of him wanted more time to gather some of the stuff up, but he had places to be, people to kill. He stopped at the doorway to the apartment, taking one last drag, before flicking the burning ganja at the bodies on the ground. Lonny was beginning to stir, coughing slightly as he inhaled the pungent smoke. Angelo grinned slightly and shut the door with a grin, making sure it locked in place. He glanced at his watch, pulled his Ray-Ban sunglasses from his pocket, and practically skipped down the steps to the back alley to wait for the show to begin.

~

Hadi stretched after the ride from the Bean to the 13th Hour. While the bike was fast, he didn't like feeling like he was about to fly off. It felt odd being back at the bar. So much had happened in such a short time. He went to the door on instinct, but James stopped him, shaking his head.

"We're here for your brother and Lindy," he mumbled.

"And my stuff," Hadi added. What he would give for a hit of white powder right now. James only rolled his eyes, knowing how Hadi was, and lead the way to the back door. It was early enough for traffic to be calm. A few garbage trucks and taxi cabs, people going to and from local areas or running their weekend errands. Even on a Saturday, things were still a little too quiet. Many of the buildings were soot stained, some of them completely empty because of structural damage. Hadi had done that.

"Come on," James said, peeking out of the alley. "We can't loiter long. They *are* still following us."

Hadi nodded and jogged along to catch James up. They took the stairs, silent but comfortable with each other. The tension that had built up between them was gone.

"Jesus, your whole building hittin' the ganja today or something?" James asked. Hadi hadn't noticed the smell until James mentioned it, but shrugged in response. The tenants above the 13th Hour were not the most upstanding citizens in the world. They weren't the worst, by any means, but they knew how to relax - except the lady that lived next door. Hadi fished his keys out of his tight pocket and unlocked the door. What he saw made his mouth drop and stomach roil.

Lonny Angram sat with Lindy's body in his arms, blood oozing to the already stained carpet from a hole between her brows. Behind them was the still form of a chocolate lab, her pink collar just barely visible behind Lonny's grieving form. The pyro-Evolved looked up when the door opened and snarled.

"Oh shit," James breathed when he saw what Hadi saw.

"This is your fault," Lonny growled as flames formed along his arms and shoulders. "My Lindsay-Rae... She's dead cuz of you!"

Hadi wanted to react, but froze. He felt panic and fear, worry. Why was this happening? Who had done this? Where was Amir?

"Hadi, move!" James cried, tugging Hadi away from the doorway as a jet of fire exploded out of the apartment. Not ten seconds later, the entire apartment blew up with an explosion so strong, both Hadi and James flew over the stair railing and down two flights of stairs, landing hard on their backs. Air rushed out of Hadi's lungs, his body protesting loudly against what just occurred.

"Up! Get up!" Hadi heard as James pulled him to his feet with the arm not in a sling, the one that kept twitching despite the medication he'd taken at the park.

"Lindy," Hadi grumbled as he coughed and stumbled behind James.

"You can't help her!" James barked, shoving Hadi forward instead of dragging. They tripped down the stairs as two more explosions tore through the building. Hadi heard others screaming, crying, panicking. People moved out onto the stairwell or cried for help from above, all of them coughing or calling for loved ones.

"Amir…" Hadi continued in a daze.

"We'll find him! Go!" James commanded. Hadi moved but didn't register much until fresh air rushed his lungs. The weak sunlight was blinding compared to the burning building. He coughed, looking around lost.

"Agent Falcon," someone said. Both Hadi and James turned to see the pyro with the bushy eyebrows pointing a gun at them. Hadi watched the man pull the trigger and flinched. His hands went up to his ears and knees flexed, but the bullet was not meant for him. Instead, it found purchase in James's chest, knocking the other man to the ground in a startling bright pool of blood that soaked his shirt and spread out beneath him.

"NO!" Hadi hollered.

"Oh get over it," Ray-Bans sighed. When Hadi turned, he was greeted with the butt end of that same gun straight to the face. He immediately dropped to the ground in a pain-filled haze that eventually turned black.

Angelo stood above Hadi Shahir's still form. He was not in any rush, calmly stowing his gun in the leather holster hidden inside his jacket. He flexed his fingers inside the leather gloves, stretching the soft, black material so it creaked. He brushed debris and chunks of ash from his black coat, even adjusted his ridiculous sunglasses before leaning down to haul Hadi up over his shoulder. The poor kid was dead weight on Angelo's shoulder, easily hefted like a rag doll but annoying all the same. It forced him to actually exert force, to *work*. He hated work, to be quite honest. He loved it, but hated it. It was an endless cycle with him.

He walked over to the car, dumping the bartender into the backseat like an unwanted coat. He checked the reflection in the window, smoothing his raven-black hair back from his face, checked for blemishes, then glanced at the bleeding body on the ground. A muffled scream and kick from the trunk reminded him of his *other* guest, forcing him to bang on the hood once more to silence the ungrateful cretin inside. The kid *could* be dead already; instead he was nice and cozy in the dark instead of out in the heat where the fire was. Angelo walked over to James Kendall and looked down with a smirk. The man had moxy, that's for sure. In another life, the two might have been decent friends, even partners. In this world, however, the middle-aged agent was well past his prime. It showed in the grays growing in the man's scruffy beard or at his temples, the crow's feet at the corner of his eyes as he coughed and squinted against the heat.

Old, injured and decrepit as he was, Kendall glared back at Angelo, choking on his own blood. His eyes were beginning to roll back into his head, but he still had the gall to glare; could've been the smoke too, but Angelo knew men like James Kendall. Smoke didn't bother men like James Kendall. People like Angelo bothered men like James Kendall. It was delicious.

"Caught your little fire bird, *Falcon*," Angelo smiled. "Your little Sparrow is next. I'll make sure she suffers. Maybe I'll even make those little brats of hers watch. Shame you won't be there to see it. Another life, perhaps. See you in Hell, Kendall. Save me a good seat."

He adjusted the lapels of his jacket once more and walked away from the dying agent. Once settled inside the car, Angelo adjusted the rear-view mirror so he could clearly see the billowing smoke and flames from the building behind him. He snorted, smirked, and snapped his fingers then put the car in gear as the entire building lit up like a match stick on the Fourth of July.

13

Hadi woke to the sensation of icicles stabbing his back and shoulders. By the time he realized there were no icicles, his entire body was numb. He shivered violently, arms tied behind his back beneath a torrent of water so cold he was positive it was being drawn directly from the arctic circle. Despite the numbness in his body, his head throbbed with constant waves of pain that nauseated him and made him incredibly dizzy. His vision blurred thanks to the water pouring over him, but he put in the effort to see his surroundings all the same. Not that there was much to see - a bare, poorly lit warehouse with high beams all rusted over or covered in bird droppings. It was large enough to make the water echo as well as the footsteps that moved toward him. He looked up, feeling the fear knot his stomach further as two, maybe three figures moved in his direction. It was difficult to tell, but no less terrifying.

"Mr. Shahir," one of the three said. The voice was odd: melodious and mechanical at the same time. Hadi blinked rapidly, hair falling into his face and water dripping into his eyes and ears. The figure was hooded but not very tall; a woman, perhaps. The person to their right was the agent with black hair and thick, bushy brows. The person between them, forced onto his knees and hands tied behind his back, was Amir. "You have a knack for being in the wrong place at the wrong time."

Hadi said nothing, shivering or trying to breathe normally as the water filled his nostrils. The figure circled him, their footsteps reverberating in a cacophony of noise until stopping once more in front of Hadi, a little closer than they were before.

"I will admit that your involvement in all of this has been both fortuitous and regrettable. You've forced my hand in a war I was not quite prepared to fight. Do you know how that makes me feel, Mr. Shahir?" the figure asked. Hadi felt like spitting on them, but settled for letting his teeth chatter instead.

"Idiotic?" Hadi answered through his chattering teeth. The answer earned him a fist to the face that put stars in his vision.

"Cute," the hooded figure chortled. "It makes me feel rushed, Mr. Shahir. I do not like being rushed. It takes the joy out of life."

Hadi looked down at the floor, unwilling to listen to the hooded figure's diatribe. He twisted uncomfortably from shivering so much, his muscles spasming painfully to try to keep him warm. That panic that he relied on to bring the fire was too overwhelming, too strong to command obedience. And, he was just too dammed wet. It was like the night in the alley, the night he tried to fight back and failed, only this time, it was worse.

"The explosions, at your place of business, for example," the figure continued. "Such a waste of a good harvest. Why? Because you had to involve the A.E.C."

The figure snapped his fingers, drawing Hadi's attention again. He heard the sobbing gasps of a woman and the wails of a baby that made his marrow turn to ice. Ray-Bans held his phone in front of Hadi's face.

The screen was split between a live feed of Nima and her daughter, and an image of James in the alley, still and pale. Hadi could not tell if that was a live feed or not, for there was not enough life in the elder man to give him that hint. Hadi felt tears stinging his eyes and shook his head.

"Don't," Hadi pleaded. Or, rather, attempted to plea. The noise his voice made was pathetic and weak; a staccato croak that tried to form intelligible thought. "Please… they didn't do anything to you."

"They did not," the figure agreed. "As I said, a regrettable crossing of paths. But also fortuitous. You find yourself in the unique position of holding information that very few have."

Hadi looked at Amir then back at the phone. Nima tried to calm her daughter with no success. They were in a gray room with flickering fluorescent lights like the shitty ones in the laundromat that needed constant replacing. Hadi saw no one else. Where was Saleh?

"What do you want?" Hadi asked again through chattering, clacking teeth.

"The PeaceKeepers, Mr. Shahir," the hooded figure said calmly, spreading their arms as if it was not truly as important as the figure was implying. "You have seen their technology, sat among them, listened to their conversations, seen where they hide."

Hadi looked at his brother and then at the figure with a confused frown on his face. He didn't know those people or their secrets. The closest he got to their tech was the bike *James* stole, and the only conversation he'd had - if it could even be called a conversation - was with that Valkyrie woman with the wings and crazy sword. That was about as helpful as Hadi could be, but that was not what the hooded figure wanted. They wanted more; they wanted detail and dirt - things Hadi did not have.

"I don't know their secrets," Hadi stuttered while shaking his head. The water beneath him was beginning to pool, creeping closer to Amir's knees. He tried to scoot away but was shoved further into the icy water, wrenching him into a contorted position that brought a cry of pain from his lips. "Leave him alone!"

He felt a whip crack across his cheek that made another explosion of stars burst onto his field of vision. Amir tried to speak on his behalf but earned similar treatment, grunting in pain from what Hadi could make out.

"I do not take kindly to commands, Mr. Shahir," the hooded figure continued calmly. Definitely a woman. Bitch. She pulled a gun from inside the folds of her long coat and pressed the barrel to Amir's head. "Your brother, for the PeaceKeepers."

"Please, don't," Hadi stammered again, then shook his head. "I don't know. Some... some chick in leather armor is the only one I know. I don't know where! I don't know their secrets! Please!"

"That's not very helpful, Mr. Shahir. Warlock."

Hadi watched the screen, purposely put in his field of vision by the asshole with the Ray-Bans. It dragged Amir closer, if momentarily. Nima cried as Saleh was shoved at her from somewhere unseen and Farah ripped from her arms. The baby wailed, wriggling in the arms of a masked figure.

"Please..." Hadi sobbed. He was ignored. Saleh was shot first, Nima and Farah both screaming. Then, Nima was silenced and the baby left wailing on her mother's corpse.

"Why are you doing this!" Hadi screamed. The burn came back, twisting his stomach, throbbing against his palm or between his shoulder blades.

The trigger cocked back, but there was no further explanation. Hadi twisted violently in his seat, water splashing everywhere, steam rising off his shoulders.

He watched Ray-Bans follow the little white plumes upward, watched Amir do the same, but continued to beg.

"I don't know!" Hadi hollered, fighting the bounds until he was hopping in the chair that held him down. "I swear I don't know! Please!"

"Last time, Mr. Shahir," the figure continued, clearly losing her patience with him. "Where are the

PeaceKeepers?"

Hadi could only shake his head and look at Amir. Amir looked at him, worry and fear in his eyes but odd resignation too. He knew what was coming, probably even knew why. Amir was smart, had so much ahead of him. *Had.* They both knew it was coming.

"I'm sorry," Hadi croaked. It took less than a heartbeat after for the gun to fire. Amir collapsed in a pool of brain matter and blood that leaked into the drain beneath Hadi's feet. He was aware of yelling, screaming until his throat was hoarse but little else until feeling heat. It was everywhere, all-consuming. The screaming ceased being his own and started resonating from the man with the Ray-Bans who turned to run; the man who'd killed Lindy and James, and countless others.

Hadi refused to let him go, directing his rage at him and him alone. The flames brought down iron beams and melted them into twisted piles of molten metal. The hooded woman vanished into the smoke. The water no longer felt like ice, but rather like lava pouring down Hadi's back.

Eventually, Hadi realized that his hands were free, though he could not recall how or why. He moved in a daze to Amir's body and carried him out of the warehouse as the entire building - the entire city - went up in flames.

~

News reports cycled through the fires that tore through half of Chicago the week before Mother's Day. Hundreds of people were injured, twenty confirmed dead, billions of dollars in damage. It was part of the horrendous acts of a serial arsonist that would later go down as one of the worst in Chicago's history. Protesters marched to city hall, demanding justice, demanding safety from the 'freaks' that made such horrible things happen. More hate crimes were being committed daily, all of them against innocent men and women, even children that the angry populace deemed to be 'abnormal'. James watched it all in disgust from the stiff new couch in an apartment that still smelled like new paint. He sat with a tumbler full of bourbon and five dossiers spread out on the matching coffee table. Everything was so… sterile. There were no personal touches, no mismatched pillows, or crooked picture frames on the wall, no comfy recliner; no Gen licking his bare toes. He hated it.

James downed the contents of the tumbler and then refilled it from a bottle at the corner of the coffee table. He set the bottle down, rubbing his chest with a grimace before grabbing his phone. Valerie continued to check in on him like she was his mother. He sent her a quick update, giving textual proof that he was still, in fact, alive, then punched a number into the cellphone and brought it to his ear while taking a long drag off a cigarette held precariously between two fingers while recollecting the tumbler of bourbon. He needed more hands. His left arm was still in a sling and he wore a brace on his knee like the old man he was, plus the dull ache in his chest from the long line of stitches that were needed to remove the bullet Angelo had been so kind to gift to him. Ass. He wanted to feel better knowing that the idiot did not actually make it out of the warehouse where the fires originated, but such unadulterated hatred just wasn't part of who James was.

IT'S HAZE. LEAVE A MESSAGE, the recording stated. There were so many messages from James he was positive the entire thing was full of his voice. He left at least one a day since being released from the hospital but never got a response back.

"Hadi, it's James. Please call me. I need to know you're ok. I need... Just call, ok?"

He hung up and threw the phone on the couch beside him. The new refill of bourbon was downed in a single gulp then refilled again. He changed the channel to something less caustic, settling on a mockumentary about mermaids. He enjoyed his cigarette and bourbon while looking over the dossiers. They were all Evolved that managed to drag themselves onto the 'wanted' list. Virgil Krisken aka "Crush" was one of them. Hadi, now being dubbed "Hellfire", was another; neither had been seen since the fires.

The buzzing beside him nearly made James drop his tumbler. As it was, he spilled bourbon all over himself and two photos. He cursed under his breath and grabbed the phone, slamming his thumb on the green button four times before it actually answered.

"Hadi?" he said expectantly. When it was not, he sagged. "No, I have not heard from him, Agent Z. -Yes, ma'am. - - One hour."

James hung up and let his head hang back. Well, at least she'd given him time to recover before pulling him under fire for his little stunt with her bike. At least he wouldn't have to look at the stupid dossiers anymore. He

closed them, cleaned up the spilled bourbon, and stood
to go change his shirt when the phone vibrated again. He
sighed, leaning over to pick it up without looking at the
screen.

"Falcon."

"The name doesn't suit you, Jimbo."

James frowned, not immediately familiar with the
voice. "Hadi?"

"He doesn't want to talk to you, Agent Kendall."
The voice was a little gruff, pitched low, but definitely one
James was familiar with. Virgil.

"V? God, Virgil, where are you? Wha-"

"We're safe. You won't be able to find us. The
phone can't be traced so don't try. We just wanted you to
know that we're safe."

"V wait a minute, please don't hang up, ok, just…
tell him I'm sorry. Please? Will you do that for me? Will
you tell him?" James begged. Silence. "Virgil?"

"Yeah," Hadi said on the other end. "Me too. Bye,
James."

14

James eyed the hologram that stood beside him in the elevator at PeaceKeeper headquarters. Somehow, it felt odd going *down* into the bowels of the city rather than *up* to a higher point in Prison Tower, as the Chicago field office had been dubbed. That God awful building was blessedly shut down as a direct result of the fire fiasco and scheduled for demolition in order to 'preserve secrecy'. Bullshit. Secrecy was lost the second Angelo set foot among their ranks. How long had he been a mole? It was something they would never learn, James wagered, despite intense investigation. All of Illinois now fell under the Milwaukee field office jurisdictions and a small contingent of PeaceKeepers - James hadn't realized how large *that* organization was until recently either - were left behind under cover to monitor the comings and goings inside of Chicago proper. Still, the hologram made James uncomfortable. It was of a boy, no older than twelve, in Victorian era dress complete with page-boy cap and suspenders. When the elevator stopped, the boy turned to regard him with a placid grin and too-large eyes. He freaked James out.

"The PeaceKeepers will take you in conference room six, Agent Falcon," the little creep said, his voice sweet but slightly mechanical. James offered a grimacing grin and stepped out. Much like the Chicago field office, everything was white, technologically advanced, and boring as all get out. His last visit was too brief for him to recall many details except how bloody white everything was. Such an odd color to choose for the building, considering how often the elite team of Evolved must come in injured.

Maintenance must be a real bear, James thought as he walked along the hall, noting the screens that popped up when he passed them. Each one displayed a number as well as a seating arrangement with occupant count and whereat the table, those occupants were. Two of the rooms were occupied, the glass frosted over for privacy. James only shook his head and proceeded to room number six.

He raised his hand to knock, but heard the hiss of the door pressurizing as it opened. It was very... *Star Trek* in nature without any of the color. Inside the room was a horseshoe-shaped table with thirteen men and women sitting around it. Zephyr sat in the middle, her chair slightly elevated above the others. James only knew Ronin, the woman in black, and Neurophage, a man in his early thirties with wire-rimmed glasses and flaming red hair. He'd seen a few others during the catastrophe with the trains. The others simply stared. The older gentleman that invaded James's brain space stood behind Zephyr rather than sitting with the rest of the team. Interesting. Slightly terrifying, but interesting.

"Sit down, Agent Falcon," Zephyr instructed, though there was no chair for him to sit in. He glanced around all the same and moved into the center of the room. *Then* the chair appeared, hissing its way up out of the floor behind him. He watched it, looked at the assembled team, and finally took a cautious seat as if expecting the thing to sink back down into the ground beneath his weight. It did not.

"I have to say, I was expecting a court marshal, not a firing squad," he mumbled wanting to get this over with. Valerie already looked at homes out in California where she was being re-stationed. He'd visited the Golden State a few times when he was out in Arizona; it was nothing impressive. Zephyr arched a brow, however, and smirked.

"Firing squad?" she echoed, highly amused. "You stole a bike, Agent Falcon. That is hardly worthy of a firing squad."

James frowned slightly, but remained silent. He observed the team, all of them doing the same to him.

Zephyr had a dossier in front of her, then proceeded to throw a projection up onto the wall behind her. The table in front of the team lit up in a similar manner, presumably with copies of the projection in smaller form displayed before each member. On the projection was a picture of Valerie, Patrick, their kids, and James. It was taken three months before Patrick passed.

"Valerie Banrae," Zephyr said, reading off the dossier. "Three children, widowed. Lives with… her mother. Relocating to California due to circumstances in Chicago. Still listed as your next of kin."

Zephyr looked up, studying him. James remained placid. This had nothing to do with Chicago, whatever *this* was. He cleared his throat and shifted in the uncomfortable white space-chair that grew out of the floor. The image shifted again. This time, it displayed a younger version of himself with his arm thrown around another gentleman, both of them in desert fatigues with a camel in the background. Iraq. The other gentleman died protecting James during their last tour together.

"War veteran," Zephyr continued. "Served two tours of duty. Honorably discharged for medical reasons and recruited to the A.E.C. shortly thereafter."

The projection changed again. This time, it was a picture from the 13th Hour. All the staff - Moose, Lindy, Haze, and Tam - their regulars like Virgil and Greg, and the guy that ordered fish sandwiches on Fridays whose name James never learned, all waved and smiled. Even Gen sat among them. Amir took the picture. James had been in town for four weeks. The picture was to commemorate his inclusion into the 'Chicago family'. He looked down at his lap, leg bouncing with agitation.

"Tamara Marshall and her son have been relocated to a safe house in Utah," Zephyr said, drawing James' attention back up to the table. "Greg Haskel has been sent to a halfway house in Georgia near his family - which, I doubt anyone knew he had given how often he was at that bar - - did you know he ran up a three *thousand* dollar tab in one week?"

James did not know. Zephyr continued.

"I want you to know, Agent Falcon, that what happened to the people who worked there is regrettable and entirely *not* your fault. Your intervention allowed us to move Joseph Marshall to the safe house in Utah; that matters. Virgil and Hadi both, are still alive if annoyingly absent. That, also, matters. You showed a great deal of compassion for human beings that are not generally given that sort of treatment. Such a thing is commendable, and, quite frankly, exactly what we're looking for."

"I'm not being court marshaled," James said finally when Zephyr was done speaking. Zephyr smiled.

"Not today, Agent Falcon," she replied. "I find myself in a unique position. Karma has chosen to step aside and be more administrative in his duties with the Peace-Keepers than an active member. Which leaves an empty slot."

James blinked, looking at the elder gentleman that looked eerily like Zephyr the more he looked at the two together. He looked at the others: at Ronin, all in black with slanted, piercing eyes and another woman with neon blue hair that reminded him of Valerie in features. He looked at the gentlemen, all regarding him man to man from seats of power and strength, weighing him for worth and felt his chest tighten painfully under such scrutiny.

"Are…" he began but could not finish the thought because the thought was ludicrous. He was old. He was banged up and sick and… She could not possibly be serious!

"I suggest altering your next of kin, Agent Falcon," Zephyr said. "Things can get… complicated inside the Strongholds."

James had nothing to say, his mouth working in silent shock.

"I think that means yes," Karma added, smiling at James as he gaped like an idiot. Oh yeah, real quality superhero material he was.

"Yes," he stammered, then cleared his throat. "Yes."

"Welcome to the team, Agent Falcon," Zephyr said. "Now, about that pesky medical issue…"

"What?"

~

Hadi stared at the water lapping up against the shoreline. It licked large rocks and washed back out into the great expanse of blue on a wave of white froth. 'La JoLa', Virgil called it, purposely mispronouncing the name just to grate at Hadi's sensitive ears for the written and spoken word. Despite his horrid accent, Hadi *could* speak Spanish rather well. He also knew how to properly pronounce every city in the great United States despite the place being all together less than spectacular. La Jolla was beautiful, however, a quiet haven of serenity that was much needed after the chaos of Chicago. He rubbed at his nose, the tip of it cold thanks to the afternoon breeze. The inside tickled, burning slightly from the sniff he'd taken before walking out to the beach. The euphoria washed over him like the waves washed over the rocks, helping him to forget.

HELLFIRE

He glanced down at the phone in his hand out of habit. Every day he stared at it, dialed a number he knew he could not reach, then shut the phone down. Sometimes, he would dial a number he knew he *could* reach, hear a voice he *knew* would bring some comfort or familiarity to the tumultuous turnings of his life, but then quickly squashed that notion as well. It was not *his* phone, not really, though MJ had done an admirable job making it *look* like his old phone to give him a bit of comfort. She had also railed on him for almost thirty minutes about *not* contacting anyone outside of their very small, very intimate little circle of 'friends' - which meant herself, Virgil, and a girl from East L.A. that helped them get set up in La Jolla shortly after their arrival. Friend of a friend, Virgil had said. Connie was nice enough and liked to tease Hadi when he was in one of his 'hazes'. He didn't mind, it was a nice distraction.

A giant beast of a dog languished in the rocky sand beside him, periodically lifting his big head to look over at Hadi. Virgil brought him home less than two weeks prior. Home, it was a word Hadi was not familiar with anymore, not really.

The phone buzzed in his hand, playing an annoying tune that told him who was calling. MJ. He shook his head but grinned all the same. He liked MJ. She reminded him of Amir, may he rest in peace. Hadi shoved that thought away, feeling the lump forming in his throat. He swallowed it down before answering, bringing the phone to his ear which, for some reason, signaled the dog to stand.

"Zeus sit down," Hadi said even as he brought the phone to his ear. "Yeah, MJ?"

"We're go for supply collection," she said, her voice blaring out into the open air and directly into Hadi's ear drum. He flinched, thumbing the volume down a great deal before bringing the phone back to his ear.

"Yeah, I'm here. - - No, you screamed into my ear. Why did you put this thing up so loud? - - I do so answer it! - - Whatever, where are V and Connie?"

He received directions and a location. A distraction was required, nothing big, but enough to pull the first responders to the location he'd been given, rather than where V and Connie waited. There was a rendezvous point for when the job was complete, and ice cream sundaes, or so MJ said. She always had ice cream sundaes after a heist - or brownies with hashish in them, or rum cakes in tiny ramekins. The girl was an insane baker, already eyeballing a place downtown for a shop. This was his life now: mercenary for hire in a weird family of other mercs and weirdos that didn't fit in anywhere else. They weren't *bad* per se; no one ever got hurt during their jobs, not on purpose anyway. Virgil liked to equate them to Robin Hood and his Merry Men. MJ said they were like Han Solo and Chewie with extra people. Hadi liked that reference better.

He glanced at the watch on his wrist, the one Amir used to wear all the time. It was their grandfather's watch, the first thing the man purchased with money he earned as a boy. It was on Amir's wrist when he died.

Now Hadi had it. MJ checked on his parents and sister periodically to make sure they were still safe. They took little Farah after the incident in Chicago, after they collected Amir's body for proper burial; there'd been nothing left to collect of Saleh and Nima. MJ made a good show of erasing Hadi from existence for their benefit, even changed his name: Nadir Adrienne. Hadi didn't care much for it, so everyone just continued to call him 'Haze'.

"Yes, I'm listening, geeze," he said. Zeus stood again, licking his face. "Zeus! Seriously, how did *I* get stuck taking care of V's dog? - - I do not need an emotional support animal, MJ. - - I hear you. - - Two hours. They better be on time this time or I'm setting V's pants on fire. Stopping for street corn is not a valid excuse to be leaving me hanging. Literally. Do you hear me? - - I'm not kidding, MJ. - - What's for dinner? - - Ew. Pass. - - See you in a few hours."

Hadi ended the call then looked at the dog. He was big and slobbery, hairy, *exactly* something Virgil would find adorable. The dog wasn't even full grown yet and already reached Hadi's waist at the shoulder. Zeus tried to lick Hadi's face again, yipping slightly when he was shoved to the side instead to avoid the slobber. Hadi didn't have time to change because of dog drool. Dog drool smelled anyway.

"Crazy mutt," Hadi said, rubbing the dog's head. He paused, looking back at the water again. He shut his eyes and said a little prayer like he always did before a job. He prayed for peace; prayed for forgiveness; prayed for strength to keep living. When he was finished, he stood up, shoving his hands into his pockets as the burn in the pit of his stomach began to smolder, changing the color of his hazel eyes to a bright, glowing ember. He looked down at the phone again and thumbed in a new number.

"Crush," he said into the receiver. "Pick up donuts and don't be late. - - Man, I will light you up like a smoke-stack. - - Yeah. - - Hellfire out."

INSTAGRAM

A Beyond Human Short Story

*C*lick*

No, the lights shone too brightly and reflected off the dirty window in the background; he should clean that before the next picture. Oh well.

Click

Lighting worked better, but the sheets weren't cooperating now. They needed to rumple just so or else it ruined the entire image.

Click

Now his arm blocked the logo of the hoodie he wore. A growl erupted from the back of Amir's throat as he swiped through the last twenty images on his camera roll. He deleted image after image, saving the ones that weren't as bad as the others before resetting the light, the stupid sheet, the dammed hoodie. The phone itself was top of the line, sent directly by the company free of charge. He used it for all of his photos and tagged the company in every post, earning what most would call a paltry 1% commission from every click off his link. Those clicks added up fast, however. A duck face, a sexy look, smoldering eyes, innocent boi - didn't matter what the 'look' was so long as the product in question could be seen. This one, though, was driving him up the literal wall. He was ready to *cilmb* said wall if it meant the picture would come out right. He even eyed the ceiling fan with narrowed, contemplative eyes.

And then, he heard the front door open.

The apartment should have been empty the rest of the night; Hadi picked up a second shift and then wanted to go out after. That usually meant he *stayed* out. Amir scrambled to get the photography equipment stuffed under his bed and the fur throw *off* his bed before Hadi came in. He failed.

"Amir, you home or-" Hadi said in Arabic. It was natural for them to speak in their native tongues, easily switching between Arabic and French when they were alone in the apartment. It gave them a little piece of home to hang on to. "What are you doing?"

Amir hung off the bed, arm stuffed under the mattress and foot up in the air for counter balance. He looked up at his elder brother and slid off the bed onto his shoulder with a groan. Hadi snorted.

"I thought you were working late today," Amir grumbled, this time in French as he rolled onto his back. Hadi moved to stand above him, looking down at Amir with a single eyebrow quirked up in curiosity.

"Tam sent me home. Said I can't have that much overtime," Hadi shrugged, then looked around. "What were you doing?"

"Nothing," Amir answered. He said it too quickly, adding to his brother's suspicion. His normally pristine room was a train wreck of clothes, shoes, props, mugs emblazoned with various logos and dirty laundry that he still needed to take over to Saleh. He'd been meaning to go see his cousin for over a week and not just for laundry services. Saleh was family, family was important to the Shahirs.

"Were you jerking off?"

"God, why are you so disgusting," Amir sighed, rolling up to his haunches. Hadi smirked, laughing at his own obscenities. Amir looked around the room for a magical explanation to what he'd been doing. Part of him wanted to accept the obscene thing his brother implied just to get out of the ribbing he knew would follow if he spoke the truth. Trouble was, Hadi knew better. Hadi knew Amir better than Amir did. He'd already started questioning how he was getting money to pay his half of the rent - he'd turned down Saleh's job offer, something he'd kept from Hadi for at least a month.

"Seriously, what are you doing?" Hadi asked in fluid, hauntingly beautiful French. Amir yearned to be back home in their small town with picturesque views and vineyards as far as the eye could see. While he didn't miss the work the vineyard brought on, he missed the sounds of the crickets in the morning, the scent of the dew on the grapes, the feel of the leaves in his hands as he walked through row upon row of vines. He could not learn what he wanted in France, however. Their father would never allow such things. It was expected for Amir to learn business and to take over the vineyards when their father retired because *Hadi* had already run from his duties as the eldest son. Amir merely sighed, pushing back up to his feet so he could face his brother.

Hadi stood a few inches taller than Amir. His chin was a little more square than Amir's and his hair shorter. Amir's hair fell in soft waves usually to the right side of his face. Between that and his clear sage-green eyes - so similar to Hadi's hazel ones - he'd landed the online jobs with ease.

"I take photos," Amir finally sighed, tossing his phone onto the bed in defeat.

"Of?" Hadi persisted. Amir merely blinked at him, made a face that suggested he might just throw a tod-dler-sized tantrum, and then deflated.

"Me."

Now Hadi blinked. He looked around the room, at the mess and the books, the unfinished homework and open laptop on the desk - a room typical of a college stu-dent.

"You?" Hadi asked. Amir nodded, waiting. "You take pictures of *you?* Doing what? Hanging off your bed? Are you selling nudes! You are!"

"See, this is why I don't tell you nothing," Amir growled, this time in English, throwing himself onto the bed face first.

"Anything," Hadi corrected despite sharing the

same accent and same grammatical colloquialisms. The trouble with Hadi was his intelligence. He was too smart to be working at a bar, to be idle for long. His mind moved in constant circles and odd patterns. He read book after book, listened to records and CDs, audiobooks, and podcasts. The library made a special exception just for him so he could check out more than the standard ten books per week. He read at least that many in a single day. But he worked at a bar in the crappy part of town in eastside Chicago instead of doing more. Hadi was happy where he was no matter what anyone told him he could be.

"Why do you care, anyway? Weren't you going out?" Amir whined, switching back to Arabic. Hadi shrugged.

"James is busy. Lindy's working. That concludes the list of people I want to hang out with right now."

"What about V?"

"I don't wanna have sex with V, Amir."

"You're sick," Amir sighed as he rolled onto his stomach, arms flopping out to his sides. "I take pictures and post them to Instagram. Companies send me free stuff and then pay me to advertise on my account."

"*That's* how you're getting your money!" Hadi hooted, laughing hard enough to double over. Amir glared at him, again, waiting. When Hadi collapsed onto the bed beside him, he did what any good brother would do - he shoved Hadi in the side.

"Shut up, Hadi."

"You seriously sit in here like a girl taking pictures of yourself!" Hadi roared.

"Yes! Get over it!" Amir said.

"I wanna see!" Hadi continued, reaching for Amir's phone.

"No!"

Amir snatched the device away quickly only to have his older brother tackle him down to the squeaky mattress, wrestling him for the smartphone like they were children. They both growled and kicked, rolled and bit until falling back onto the floor with grunts and shouts.

"Stop! Let it go!"

"I wanna see!"

"No!"

"Lemme see it!"

"NO!"

"Amir, let it go!" Hadi growled, this time with enough heat in his hand Amir hissed, pulling away as he dropped his phone. Hadi retrieved it with a smirk, a small orange glow in his eyes.

"You cheated!" Amir grumbled, rubbing his wrist. It bore an angry red mark in the distinct shape of a hand and fingers. The mark would be gone by morning with just a little bit of aloe or vanilla, but it angered Amir to have been so betrayed.

"I did, but you're being a prick. What are you hiding?" Hadi asked, now scrolling through the phone's gallery. Picture after picture reflected on Amir's laptop, the two connected via Bluetooth so that all the editing happened in real time with easy posting. "These are all, like, model pictures and stuff."

"Give me that," Amir finally growled, snatching

his phone back from his brother with a snarl on his face. "Go away."

Hadi chortled but threw himself on the bed above Amir's head. "Don't be that way. I get to tease you. It's my birthright."

"Asshole."

"What's all this for, anyway? You hate people. You can't even say easy words - in *any* language - when you need to talk to a girl and now you're looking all sexy with a ... what is that?"

"Sherpa."

Hadi blinked at the response, looking over Amir's shoulder in silence.

"It's nothing. It's just a thing I do to get money to pay my half of the rent."

"I thought you was working with Saleh?" Hadi said, shifting as he sat up, bare legs dangling over the edge of the bed. Amir looked at him with a frown, following his brother's outfit all the way to the neck. He wore football shorts in a color that Amir equated to a Pepsi can with a heather gray tank that read 'BITE ME' in big rainbow letters and a beanie with little red flowers on it.

"What are you wearing?" Amir dared. Hadi looked down at himself and shrugged.

"It was crazy outfit day at the bar," he explained. "I took the beanie off Lindy. You shoulda seen what Tam wore. OOF!"

Amir only blinked then looked back at his phone and sighed heavily. He knew somewhere in his mind that he should not have lied to his brother. Hadi never lied to

him, always honest and open about probably more than
Amir wanted to know. Amir was the first to know about
Hadi's Evolution, seeing the halo of it around him at a very
young age. He saw the halos around other people too - not
all people, just Evolved as he'd come to learn. Amir was
the first to hear about Hadi's sexual preferences too. Not
that the young man had *asked* but Hadi had shared anyway
describing the differences between kissing a woman and
kissing a man while Amir still *fantasized* about having the
balls to even *talk* to a woman. He'd learned early on about
Hadi's drug habit, starting with pot and then the cocaine
the young bartender still worked to kick. He'd had a good
run - a whole two weeks before falling off again. That was
probably the hardest thing to know - how much his brother
struggled to do right only to fail each time.

"I'm sorry I didn't tell you. I just… I didn't want
you to tell Saleh, I guess. Or… or tease me. It's nothing.
All they want is a few pictures with their stuff and I tag
them and then I get money anytime someone clicks the
link."

"Good money?" Hadi asked in Arabic. Amir
looked over his shoulder up at his brother and nodded.
"The lighting in here is shit."

Amir twisted himself around to look Hadi in the
eye. His elder brother smirked and looked up at the ceiling
fan then at the *one* circle light Amir had or the box set up
he'd been given to take pictures with.

"You need a better camera, too," Hadi said as he
began taking things apart and rearranging everything.

"What are you doing?" Amir dared again, standing up as if to stop Hadi. In reality he knew that was not possible. There was no stopping Hadi in anything the man set his mind to.

"Fixing the light. If you move some of the shit you've got in here and change out the standard incandescent bulbs for halogen bulbs it'll give you more white light than yellow light and then you can leave whatever that circle thing is on the desk for when you do pictures there. Plus, if you get a stabilizer on your selfie stick, it'll stop it from blurring. You had too many of those in your gallery."

Amir could only blink, listening to his brother prattle on in Arabic about photos and lights and things he *shouldn't* know. Except, it was Hadi. Of course, he knew it. He absorbed anything he read like a sponge absorbed water.

"Want me to see if I can get you a different camera or do you have to use the one on your phone?" Hadi asked as he unscrewed all the lightbulbs from the ceiling fan fixture.

"Do we even have the…" Amir began, pointing at the fan.

"Halogens? Yeah, I use them in my room. I like the light better."

Amir only rolled his eyes and chuckled. The weight of his secret lifted, letting him breathe easier since he first declined Saleh's job offer. He didn't want to be a drag on anyone, least of all his brother.

An hour later, Amir's whole room looked different. New lights were put in the fan above. A strip of LED lights was pasted up around the perimeter of the room itself and things put in strategic places for easier 'real life' selfies in the small room. Plus, Hadi pulled out a camera from his room that looked like it was worth more than their apartment.

"Where did you get that?" Amir asked as he edited some of the images he'd taken before Hadi's intrusion.

"Stephen," Hadi answered absently. It was not a name Amir recognized. "So, use this one to take pictures with when you're not tagging the phone company. It has better pixel rate. I can take them for you if you want."

"Do you moonlight as a photographer too?" Amir asked in French. Hadi looked up from the camera and blinked.

"Why do you think I have the camera?"

"You're an idiot, Hadi."

ABOUT THE AUTHOR

Michelle Schad is a shortstory author and novelist of various genres. She has work appearing in Bards and Sages online fiction magazine  and all of Corrugated Sky's current anthologies. Her debute novel, *Hellfire*, was originally published in 2018 with a new rebranding in 2020.

When not entertaining others with words, she is a tamer of the chaos created by her husband, four children, and too many pets. She is a game master of Pathfinder, D&D, and FATE campaigns, a lifetime Supernatural fan, lover of all things Eeyore, and perveyor of all things alcoholic and/or caffeinated.

You can keep up with what she does at www. tamingchaos.net, follow her on FaceBook, or stay in touch via Twitter at @ChelleSchad.

HELLFIRE

HELLFIRE